"Uh, I have ... you," Jayde ad...

Her mother smiled g... honey. Brad already ~~told us the good news.~~ She reached out to stroke Jayde's cheek. "And although we don't like these fainting spells you're having, we couldn't be happier for you."

That threw her. Jayde sat up in bed. "You couldn't?"

"Of course not... Although it was a shock when Brad first told us. I hadn't thought you'd ever do such a thing," her mother chided softly.

Shame for having lied to her parents, especially about her supposed "marriage" to her boss, made Jayde lower her gaze. "I'm so sorry, Mom."

"Oh, now, honey, it's not the end of the world," her mother soothed. "These are modern times, after all. Still, I don't mind saying that your daddy was a little upset. But you're sitting pretty now; that's all that matters."

Was her mother saying that her lies were okay? That didn't sound like the mother Jayde knew. "Mom, what are you talking about?"

"About the baby, of course."

The baby? What baby?

Dear Reader

What better job could we hope for than to get paid for sitting around the house? Just kicking back and daydreaming by the pool. Actually, that's how some people interpret what I do for a living as an author. And they're right, but don't tell them, will you? They'd just be jealous.

So, after writing, my dream job would be as a house-sitter to the rich and famous. There I'd be, all alone in a tropical climate somewhere, just me and the furniture, with books to read, a car and money at my disposal, living the high life...until everything went wrong at once. Wait a minute...that's not my life. That's what happens to Jayde Green, the heroine of this book—but she handles it about the way I would. Read her story...then ask yourself if you'd do anything differently.

Because...it could happen to you!

Enjoy,

Cheryl Anne Porter

SITTING PRETTY

BY
CHERYL ANNE PORTER

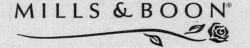

MILLS & BOON®

To Etheleen and Bill Oster,
sitting pretty out there in Bartow, Florida.

First published in Great Britain 2002
Harlequin Mills & Boon Limited,
Eton House, 18-24 Paradise Road, Richmond, Surrey TW9 1SR

© Cheryl Anne Porter 2000

ISBN 0 263 82959 6

Set in Times Roman 10½ on 12 pt.
01-0802-46813

Printed and bound in Spain
by Litografía Rosés, S.A., Barcelona

1

THE FADING WAIL of the ambulance siren deepened the already deathly silence that held in its grip the shocked front-office staff of the Homestead Insurance Company. The scene more resembled a corporate-world Stonehenge than it did the normally tidy and efficient Kansas City-based headquarters. Around the room, desks were scattered in disarray, having been shoved aside by paramedics hastening to get to the victim. Drops of blood—Mr. Homestead's blood—dotted the carpet.

Big-haired, bespectacled, and beside herself, Mrs. Lattimer stood in front of Jayde's desk. "This is the last straw, Ms. Greene. You've worked here a total of three months, and those three months have been marked with one harrowing incident after another—all of your making."

Jayde grimaced. "Well, I wouldn't say it was *all* that bad—"

"You wouldn't?" Mrs. Lattimer shrieked. "You have been nothing but trouble. In October, it was the water cooler. Then in November, it was the janitor. Somehow we all managed to get through December unscathed. But now this—"

"Okay, the water cooler *was* my fault," Jayde admitted. "Although, stuck out there in the hallway like it was, anybody could have tripped over it. It just happened to be me. And, if you ask me, the carpet needed cleaning, anyway. But the janitor wasn't my fault. Well, not in principle. The man should not sneak up on people who are working late.''

"Mr. Rosario was not sneaking, Ms. Greene. He was mopping.''

"Exactly. But in the women's washroom. Inside a stall. It was like…there I was, and then, poof, there he was. I did what any—''

"You yanked his mop out of his hands and beat him on the head with the handle.'' Mrs. Lattimer crossed her chunky arms over her bosom and raised an eyebrow. "He suffered a concussion and spent Thanksgiving in the hospital.''

Jayde raised her chin defiantly…and a bit guiltily. "I said I was sorry for that. And I did take a home-made pie to his family, remember?''

She nodded. "I do. It made them all sick. Mr. Rosario quit right after that. He remains convinced you tried to kill him and his entire family.''

Jayde exhaled tiredly. "Look, I'm sorry about Mr. Rosario, I really am. And the water cooler. But what do those have to do with today and Mr. Homestead? I just don't—''

"Allow me to tell you, then,'' Mrs. Lattimer interrupted. "You have three strikes against you, that's what. And that means you're fired. You are no longer my assistant. I will contact the employment agency that sent you and tell them they can expect your final paycheck in two weeks. But right now, you are to gather your belongings and leave the building immediately.''

Jayde's cheeks burned with embarrassment as she stood up, preparing to do as she'd been ordered…in front of a roomful of very quiet employees. Tension and sympathy seemed to flavor the heated air flowing from the vents overhead. Jayde had befriended several of the women here, but she certainly didn't expect any of them to stand up for her in this instance. Besides, there was nothing they could do. They knew, as Jayde did, that Mrs. Lattimer had wanted Jayde gone from the moment Mr. Homestead first laid his womanizing eyes on her. And now apparently she was to be gone.

But not quite yet. Mrs. Lattimer wasn't finished with her. "Under the circumstances, young lady, you should be glad that all we've done is fire you. You should be arrested for assault. If it weren't for Mr. Homestead's wishes, which he made plain—before he passed out—you would be. If it were up to me, I'd already have you locked up and the key thrown away."

Jayde didn't doubt it for a moment. The woman was a jealous dragon. "It was an accident, pure and simple, Mrs. Lattimer. You know that—" Just as Jayde knew that Mrs. Lattimer, a widow, was secretly sweet on the very married Mr. Homestead. "—and I told Mr. Homestead I was sorry—"

"You seem to think that a simple 'I'm sorry' will clear up everything—including assaults on people and equipment—Ms. Greene. Well, it won't. Besides, I doubt the dear, sweet man heard you, considering he was unconscious. But it doesn't matter. You're fired, and you're to leave this instant."

Her heart pounding, her hands clenched in dread for her immediate future, Jayde could only stare at her boss. Well, her boss's secretary. Okay, her *former* boss's secretary. Apparently, the man didn't have the guts to fire her himself. Jayde swallowed guiltily. The truth was the man barely had *any* guts left at all…because she had just, well, run him through. One erratic and fateful swing of her arm with a letter opener. How was she to know the darned stubborn sticky manila envelope would give at the exact moment that Mr. Homestead was coming up behind her desk? People, including janitors, should announce themselves.

Still, it wasn't as if she didn't feel badly about what had happened. She'd been hysterical and had even tried to staunch the flow of blood from Mr. Homestead's big belly. Unfortunately, compounding the disaster, only important company documents had been close at hand.

So, in less time than she would have thought possible, Jayde found herself on the icy street. Frozen emotionally as well as physically, she clutched the small plastic trash bag into which she'd stuffed the few personal belongings she'd kept at work. Nestled amongst the tissues and lipstick was a cheaply framed picture taken last month of her family around their Christmas tree. The only face missing from the photo was Jayde's own.

And now, here it was, the middle of January, and she had ten dollars to her name. Yes, she'd sent too much money home to Kentucky for Christmas gifts. She'd known it then, and she knew it now. But how could she not have, with three younger sisters and two even younger brothers to buy for? Not to mention her parents. She knew they wouldn't spend a dime on themselves…so she'd tucked in small gifts for them with her check. They'd wanted her to use the money to come home for a visit. Jayde would have loved that, too. But she knew better. The kids needed new shoes and coats more than they needed to see her.

Her phone call to them on Christmas Day had proven that. Hearing how happy they were with their new clothes had been Jayde's present to herself. She sighed. The only thing the Greenes ever had in abundance was love. Her parents worked hard, but without education and marketable skills, they didn't have a chance to even break even. So, even though their pride suffered, they depended on Jayde's monthly contributions. She knew that. And she was happy to send what money she could. It wasn't much, because she was still paying back the loan she'd taken out when she'd been accepted two years ago at the prestigious Kansas City School of Art and Design...from which she'd flunked out recently.

Don't go there, girlfriend, she warned herself. *You had to attend classes, work a forty-hour week and somehow find time to paint. You were killing yourself with that routine. Something had to give.* Jayde's expression threatened to crumple. She wiped at her eyes, fighting against the tears threatening to spill over. *Okay, but did it have to be school that crashed?* She'd loved it. Every minute. There she was, the first Greene to attend any institution of higher learning. Her whole family had been so proud. And look what had happened. She'd flunked out. *That doesn't mean you can't be a successful artist.* Jayde made a scoffing sound. *Yeah, right. You flunk out of art school and go on to be a great artist. It happens every day. A great example I am. "Just watch me," I said to the kids. Yeah, right. Just watch me freeze to death standing here on this corner.*

Shivering and ready to chuck her lifelong dream of

being an artist, Jayde stamped her feet to get the circulation going in them. She had to figure out what she was going to do next…besides feeling sorry for herself, that is.

But all she seemed able to do was to torture herself with her shortcomings. This wasn't the first time she'd lost a really good job. The one she'd had before joining Homestead Insurance had been yanked out from under her, too. How could she forget *that* day last September?

She and about two hundred other people had been let go, without warning, from the restaurant-supply company they'd all worked for. It had just suddenly been shut down. By the FBI. Embezzlement, she'd heard. Top management had gone to jail, and the rest of them—the innocent, unsuspecting employees—had gone either to the unemployment office or, like Jayde, back to one of the various employment agencies around town.

And now she was unemployed…again. Could it be worse?

It began to snow. *Well, you ask a question…* Totally demoralized now, Jayde raised her face to the oppressive gray sky. Big, fat, wet flakes gently assaulted her, melting like tears on her face. It seemed even Mother Nature wanted to take a shot at her. Jayde exhaled sharply. Standing here and freezing to death was getting her nowhere fast. She looked up and down the street, as if an answer to her dilemma would suddenly come lightly tripping by. But all she saw were people scurrying from one place to the next. No doubt *employed* people.

Feeling alone as she never had before, Jayde tried to put a brave face on her situation. *She* certainly wasn't among the employed right now, so she didn't need to be standing here in the cold and the snow with all the poor working slobs, now did she? Heck, she could even avoid rush hour by catching a bus and going home. Home was a tiny studio apartment in which she could curl up with a hot drink. It sounded lovely. But then, her snug little scenario crashed with her next thought. Home was where she could also cry over her slim options and the even slimmer balance in her checkbook.

Switching her bag of belongings to her other hand, she rubbed distractedly at her forehead, a part of her brain noting that her bare fingers were freezing. *What am I going to do? I have no money, no car, no family here, no real friends to speak of, a loan to repay, and no money for rent.* Jayde knew that her last paycheck from Homestead, the one Ms. Lattimer was forwarding to the employment agency, would be applied to her outstanding placement fee there. Which meant she'd have no money for rent or groceries. She'd be homeless. Unless a miracle came from up above.

Could it?

Jayde looked up again at the gunmetal-gray sky. No miracles. Only snow. Lots of snow. Jayde quirked her mouth, deciding she'd make her own miracle happen. But first, she needed to get across town to see the irrepressibly snooty Ms. Kingston. Jayde swallowed hard, thinking of the young, chic and snobby placement counselor at the employment agency—which Ms. Kingston also owned. The woman wasn't the least bit friendly, but she was efficient and had certainly found Jayde two jobs already in the year she'd been in Kansas City. Maybe the woman was good for one more.

Great. I get a guardian angel with an attitude.

Half-frozen, feeling as low as she ever had, Jayde approached the knot of huddling people at the bus stop and looked down the street. Of course, the bus was nowhere in sight. And, with the way her luck had been going, Jayde wasn't surprised when the wind picked up and the snow changed to stinging ice pellets. She snuggled down into her inadequate coat as best she could and tried to sort through her problems one by one. The most immediate one, of course, was that she was slowly turning into a Popsicle—an unemployed Popsicle. She couldn't make her rent and she couldn't go home. But the worst thing was that she was no closer to realizing her dream of becoming a successful artist. But, darn it, how could she be? It wasn't as if she'd ever had the opportunity to indulge her desire to paint. Desire? It was way beyond desire. It was destiny. It was what she'd been born to do, just like Picasso or Monet or even Grandma Moses. She could feel it. Truly feel it. Deep down inside.

Vibrant images filled her head, just as canvases and paints crowded her studio apartment. Painting with oils. It was the one and only thing she truly wanted to do. Why was she given this desire if she wasn't supposed to do something with it? An ironic smile claimed Jayde's mouth. Well, maybe she *was* making progress. After all, now that she'd lost her job, she could officially become a starving artist. That was progress, right? Her smile faded. How could she paint when she couldn't even keep a roof over her head and food in her belly…which chose that moment to growl.

Jayde clutched at her coat, pressing her fisted hand against her stomach. Just then, the crowd around her quickened to life. She looked down the street. A lumbering city bus slowly but blessedly wheezed its way toward them. Taking that as a sign of better things to come, Jayde found herself suddenly overcome with a sense of well-being. The bus was coming, she'd get another, better job, maybe at an art museum, and she'd have the money to paint wonderful pictures. And then people would clamor to buy her Impressionistic renderings of Kansas City's unique fountains, her true passion and the reason she'd moved here in the first place.

And then she'd have the life she wanted, and she'd give her family everything they needed—and things would be okay. It could and would happen…if only Ms. Kingston didn't throw her out the minute she walked through the door—yet again—of Your Dream Job Employment Agency.

''YOU AGAIN.''

Jayde swallowed nervously and felt her smile slip a notch. Since she hadn't yet been invited in, she stood in the doorway of the warm and plush office she'd been escorted to by the receptionist, Tasha. Like everyone else in this place, the young girl had a way of making Jayde feel no better than the doormat she'd just wiped her feet on. She didn't like that feeling. After all, she was a paying client here and not a beggar…at least, not yet. Striving to seem cheery, Jayde said, ''Yes, ma'am. Me again. How are you, Ms. Kingston?''

Ms. Kingston…with no small show of resignation…removed her wire-rimmed glasses and put down the file she'd been reading. The slender woman, her short red hair fashionably cut, frowned. ''I've asked you repeatedly not to call me ma'am. I'm the same age you are.''

Well, she sure didn't seem as though she was twenty-five. In fact, to Jayde, she didn't seem to have any age at all. She'd never been able to picture Ms. Kingston doing anything like cooking or dating or watching TV or visiting family—or having any problems. Much less a first name. In Jayde's mind, the woman's name was Ms. Kingston and she only existed here in this office. ''Yes, ma'am—oh, I'm sorry. You just asked me not to—''

''Mrs. Lattimer has already called me.'' The woman's blue eyes resembled ice chips.

Jayde's heart thumped heavily. ''I see. Then you know why I'm here.''

''Of course. I expected you. You may as well come in and sit down.'' Ms. Kingston indicated a chair across from her desk.

Jayde entered and sat. Perched on the edge of the cushion, she felt totally inadequate. As she watched as Ms. Kingston raised a mug of steaming coffee to her lips, a chill chased through her, making Jayde wish she had such warmth rushing through her own cold body. She couldn't look away, not even when Ms. Kingston caught her staring.

The woman thunked her mug down atop the blotter on her desk and pursed her lips. ''I suppose you'll want a cup. Although, I don't know if there's any coffee left at this late hour. But I can have Tasha see if—''

''No, thank you. I'm fine.'' Jayde's stubborn pride rose up. ''What I would like is for you to find me another job. And quickly. Please.'' Jayde tried to smile but her facial muscles were stiff and uncooperative. Ms. Kingston continued to stare at her. Accusingly. Suddenly Jayde's pride deflated. "Look, I didn't try to kill Mr. Homestead," she blurted. "It was an accident. And the paramedics said the wound wasn't all that deep…"

Ms. Kingston managed a thin smile. "I'm sure he'll be fine." She tapped a painted nail atop the folder she'd been reading when Jayde had come in. "I have your file right here. But, tell me, Miss Greene, why do you continue to come to this agency?"

She was tempted to reply, *Because of the warm and fuzzy prison feel to the place, Warden.* Instead, she said, "Because of the name. Your Dream Job. I like that. And because I know you. And because—" Jayde looked down at her lap, at her hands knotted together atop her pathetic trash bag of belongings…and thought of her huge loan and of her family and how they needed her. This was no time for pride.

She looked up, meeting Ms. Kingston's waiting gaze, and fought the hot tears that were gathering in her eyes. "The truth? Because I don't have anywhere else to go. And my rent will be due soon. And my last paycheck from Homestead won't even cover the remaining part of your placement fee. And I don't have any choice but to ask you to find me another job that has yet another fee I can't afford—"

"Wait." Ms. Kingston held out a hand. "Spare me the angst. I think I actually have something here that might just *be* your dream job."

Jayde couldn't believe her luck. "Would it happen to be at an art museum? Because that would be a dream come true. Did I ever tell you that I paint?"

Ms. Kingston raised a perfectly plucked eyebrow. "You…paint? As in houses?"

Jayde frowned. "No. Fountains. Anybody can paint a house—oh, wait. You think I mean paint like in paint houses, a house painter. No. I mean fountains, as in, I'm an artist. A painter. You know…oils, acrylics? Things that hang in galleries and museums?"

"Oh. Of course." Ms. Kingston's smile was condescending, causing Jayde to wonder where a letter opener was when she really needed one. "How nice for you. And no, this opening isn't with an art museum or a gallery. But still, I think you're perfectly suited for it. It's even with one of our best clients."

Jayde sat back warily. "One of your best clients? Then, why are you offering it to me?" No one had to tell Jayde that the woman didn't like her.

Ms. Kingston slowly ducked her chin as her eyes narrowed. She looked like a Siamese cat plotting some unsuspecting mouse's death. "Because for one thing, you don't have a job. And this client needs someone right away." Then an angry glint darkened Ms. Kingston's eyes. "He always does. The man just thinks he can snap his fingers and—" Ms. Kingston caught herself. "More to the point, I have no qualms about recommending you. You've been through our background search, been fingerprinted, bonded. And I feel you're just what he deserves in a woman—I mean, in an employee." Ms. Kingston inhaled and exhaled sharply. "I *mean,* you're squeaky clean."

Squeaky clean? Jayde decided that was probably the nicest thing Ms. Kingston had ever said to her. "Thanks."

Ms. Kingston smiled that thin smile of hers and began moving things around on her desk until she came up with what she was obviously looking for, a big index card. "Here it is." Leaning forward, her elbow planted atop her desk, she dangled the card, balancing it as if it were a cigarette between her fingers.

But to Jayde, it was the Golden Fleece, the answer to all her problems. All that, and she had no idea what type of job it was. Nor did she care. She needed a job now. "I'll take it."

Ms. Kingston made a sound that could have been a chuckle, but Jayde doubted it. "You don't even know what it is."

"I don't care what it is."

"You'd have to move."

Jayde frowned. "Move? You mean like across town or to the suburbs?"

"No. I mean like across country. This job's in Florida."

"Flor—?" Jayde could only stare at the woman. She thought of her precious fountains here, just waiting for her to paint them. They depended on her, these fountains. And she needed them. They were her passion, her ticket to success, and she wouldn't leave them. She shook her head. "I'm not moving to Florida. Look through your cards, please, and see what they might have for me here in Kansas City."

Ms. Kingston pursed her lips. "You don't seem to understand, Miss Greene. I don't have anything else for you. Except this job in Florida. Why can't you move?"

My fountains. I can't leave because of my fountains. Jayde stared at her unwitting tormentor. Her heart was breaking at the mere thought of abandoning her dream. But Jayde knew someone as practical and efficient as Ms. Kingston wouldn't understand. In fact, she'd think Jayde was nuts. And right now, Jayde had to admit, maybe she was. "So, what's so special about this Florida job?"

Looking suddenly very pleased, Ms. Kingston said, "So you'll consider leaving? Moving far away from me—I mean, from here?"

Just as she'd suspected. It was Jayde's turn to incorporate a thin smile. "Sure. If it's the right job…as you seem to think it is."

"Oh, it is. The client pays a very competitive salary, provides health care and will even pay my agency's fee. He'll also prepay your moving expenses and provide you with an airline ticket—first class, I might add. And if you accept this job, Miss Greene, I'll even waive what might be left of your outstanding fee on the Homestead job, once your last paycheck is sent to me."

"Wow," Jayde said…somewhat flatly. It did sound perfect, darn it. "What about the lease on my apartment? I just signed a new one two weeks ago."

Ms. Kingston shrugged. "Not a problem. My client will buy it out." Then she sat forward, ready, apparently, to brush away any and all of Jayde's obstacles. "Anything else that could keep you from leaving tomorrow?"

Jayde's jaw dropped. She gripped her chair's arms. "Tomorrow? Did you say tomorrow? Are you serious? There's a snowstorm out there. I'd have to pack. I'd have to—"

Ms. Kingston leaned forward, staring Jayde in the eye. "You'd have to do what—move to Florida, all expenses paid, to live in the lap of luxury, make top dollar, and have most of your time to yourself? Oh, what an awful thing I'm asking you to do, Miss Greene."

Jayde narrowed her eyes. "Oh, yeah? Then why don't you take it?"

"Because it's not me Brad wants—" Ms. Kingston turned red...carmine red, Jayde's artistic eye decided. And the woman looked angry...and insulted. "I'm not the one looking for a job, Miss Greene. I own this agency. And besides, I want nothing further to do with Brad—" She again caught herself. "It's none of your business."

"I didn't ask," Jayde said slowly, eyeing the woman across the desk from her. "But I am now. Who's Brad?"

Ms. Kingston folded her hands together atop her desk, going right back to her purring cat demeanor. "You'll find out soon enough...if you take the job."

"I might. Just tell me what the catch is."

Ms. Kingston pulled back, offended. "I don't know what you mean. There is no 'catch.'"

Cold and tired, Jayde quit playing the game and spoke her mind. "Sure there is. There always has been. Now that I think about it, you've sent me to a job that the FBI was already surveilling. And when that went south, you sent me to a job where the boss can't keep his lecherous hands off his female employees. Now you've got the perfect job for me— halfway across the country! In a blizzard. See? A catch. I mean, what does this man do? Is he a drug lord? The Mafia? What?"

Ms. Kingston chuckled. "Hardly. I would never have been involved with anyone who—" She cut herself off and gave Jayde a cold stare.

Sighing, Jayde realized she didn't have much

choice. "So...what's this job? What would I be do-ing?"

Ms. Kingston smelled victory, that much was clear. She placed the index card on her desk and smirked. "You'd be a house sitter."

Jayde did a double take. "A what?"

"A house sitter. For one of the richest men in the country, Ms. Greene."

That Brad guy, no doubt. Still, to Jayde, this whole thing sounded pretty Gothic-romance-novel to her. "A house sitter, and he's really rich. Then why does he need *you?* Wouldn't he have, well, *people* to do that?"

Ms. Kingston looked down her slender nose at Jayde. "We—my agency—*are* 'his people' for such matters, Miss Greene. I've placed sitters for him in his homes in Rome and Paris. But my client's family home is here. That's why he used me—um, uses my agency."

Jayde sat forward, ignoring all the personal slipups. So what if Ms. Kingston and this rich Brad guy had a history. Jayde had just heard three things more rel-evant to her. Rome. Paris. Kansas City. Meccas for fountains and the artists who wanted to paint them. "You're not serious? He has homes in Rome and Paris? And Florida? And right here in Kansas City? Are you sure this Brad guy doesn't need a sitter for his house here?"

"No. An old family retainer resides in his home here. What my client needs is someone in Florida. Tomorrow. And if I were you, I wouldn't call him Brad."

Jayde shook her head. "Of course not. But, wow, it's that 'tomorrow' part that's hard to accept. I mean, the packing, alone. And just trying to find a moving company in a snowstorm. I wouldn't even—''

''No problem. I'm authorized to take care of all those details for you. All you have to do is pack the clothes you want to take and get on an airplane. Everything else can be put in storage. What do you say?'' Ms. Kingston checked her diamond-studded watch, as if the offer expired in a matter of seconds. She again focused on Jayde…and waited.

The woman's cavalier attitude really angered Jayde. She ought to just take herself and her pride and get right up and walk out the door—if she wanted to be homeless and renege on her debts. Jayde forced herself to calm down and to think. Leaving Kansas City wasn't the end of her life or even her artist's dream. Because a true artist could paint anywhere. Anywhere. And *she* was a true artist.

Silently asking for courage to embark on this new plan, Jayde said, ''So, Ms. Kingston, that fabled Fountain of Youth…wasn't it in Florida?''

2

NOT BAD. Not bad at all. Bathed by warm Sarasota, Florida sunshine, Jayde stood in a huge fenced-in terra-cotta-flagstone-paved courtyard. Surrounding her was tropical greenery she couldn't even begin to name. To her left was a kidney-shaped pool. And right in the middle of the courtyard was a magnificent three-tiered Italianate fountain. She couldn't believe this. It was like a sign, one that said Welcome Home, Jayde.

Slowly now, she turned round and round, admiring the compound of her new employer, Mr. Bradford Hale. One of the richest men in the country, Ms. Kingston had said. He was no one Jayde had ever heard of. But that didn't really surprise her, considering she was just a blue-collar worker's daughter from Kentucky. Maybe Mr. Hale was a quiet, secure rich man, one who saw no need to broadcast his wealth and power. Someone of humility and values. Someone, despite Ms. Kingston's relationship with the man, whom Jayde could respect. She certainly hoped so, at any rate.

"Wow," she said aloud to the muscled hunk of a chauffeur who'd met her at the Sarasota-Bradenton Airport. "Are you sure this is the right place? I thought houses like this existed only in movies. Or maybe magazines."

"Yes, ma'am, Jayde. This is the right place."

"Boy, I'll say. But I don't think I've ever seen this style of house before. What's it called?"

"Northern Italian. Some call it Mediterranean."

"Northern Italian. Mediterranean," Jayde repeated with due reverence as she faced the tile-roofed, two-story structure finished in a warm sunset-colored stucco. She believed the house—mansion, really—with its arched entry and windowed balconies, was bigger than a horse barn. Finally, Jayde eyed the chauffeur and quipped, "I don't think I'm in Kansas City anymore, Toto."

The man chuckled. Tall, dark and handsome in a no-nonsense sort of way, and dressed in an honest-to-God chauffeur's black uniform, he had been standing in the terminal, holding up a hand-lettered sign with her name on it. He'd introduced himself as Lyle and had proven to be kind and solicitous of her every need. They'd traveled to the house in a black stretch limousine. Jayde thought she was dreaming.

But now that Jayde was standing here, she was suddenly overcome. So she blurted out the first relevant thing she could think of. "So, where is he? My boss, I mean. Will I meet him anytime soon?" Self-consciously, she pulled at her very inadequate wool skirt and knit sweater, trying as much to straighten them as she was to tug them away from her itchy skin. It must be eighty degrees here. She'd already shed as many layers of clothes as modesty would allow since stepping out of the airport terminal.

Lyle set down her bags and her artist's easel, and then searched through his pockets, presumably for a key to the house. "You'll meet him today, as it turns out. Mr. Hale will be arriving from Rome in a few hours. I'm to set you up here, show you the way things work and then go back and get him. He'll be staying here tonight and part of tomorrow. Then he leaves for England.''

Jayde was duly impressed. ''That's some life he's got there.''

Lyle grinned as he finally fished a key out. ''It keeps him busy. And pays for all this.'' He inserted the key into the lock, turned it and opened the door. ''Come on in. Welcome home.'' He stood aside for Jayde to enter. She heard a high-pitched whine, like an alarm, and sent Lyle an alarmed look. ''Go ahead,'' he urged. ''Look around. I'll carry your stuff in and deal with the security system. I've got thirty seconds to punch in the code, or the alarm sounds and JOCK calls the police.''

''Well, that's good of him...I guess.'' Whoever Jock was. Jayde stepped out of Lyle's way...and found herself in a world she'd never have believed. A feast for the senses. Across the way, ceiling-to-floor windows looked out onto a beautiful expanse of blue water. Inside, mauves and tans and greens and touches of blue greeted her. It was formal yet inviting. Exciting yet restful. Framed artwork that appeared to her to be the real thing hung on the walls. Big, bold furniture, richly upholstered accented each room. Awestruck, she wandered around the house. Not one tiny detail had gone lacking, not from the sunken wet bar to the marine fish tank that backed it. Jayde could hardly breathe. In fact, she feared she was going to cry. Being here was like winning the lottery. Things like this just didn't happen to her.

Then Lyle reminded her of his existence. ''Come on. I'll show you to your room.''

Jayde obediently followed him. Through a formal dining room, past a kitchen a professional chef would be proud of, down a hall…and into a bedroom that dazzled her. A veritable dream come true itself, complete with a queen-size bed, complete with a down comforter and a walk-in closet bigger than her entire studio apartment in Kansas City had been. Through an open doorway on the other side of the room she could see a bathroom…with a marbled countertop. She turned to Lyle. "You're pulling my leg, right? This isn't my room. This is Mr. Hale's, isn't it?"

Lyle just grinned. "No. Mr. Hale has the upstairs."

Jayde eyed him. "The upstairs? As in 'all of it,' the whole thing?"

"Yes. Besides his bedroom suite, there's a workout room, office, study, wet bar, home theater, things like that." Lyle counted them off on his fingers.

"Wow. The rich really are different." Full of wonder, she again swept her room with a glance and then pivoted to face Lyle. He was still in the doorway, watching her in a speculative sort of way, a shoulder propped against the doorjamb. Jayde felt her face coloring. "I don't believe any of this. Pinch me."

Chuckling, Lyle pushed away from the door and held his hands out defensively in front of him. "Not on your life. Now, if you don't mind, before you settle yourself in, I'd like to take a few minutes to familiarize you with the alarm system and the electronic butler."

It took a moment for his words to sink in. "Electronic butler? Like a robot?"

"No. Like a computer. He runs the whole house. He was the one I was talking to and telling to turn on the lights, things like that, just now."

"Oh." Earlier, she'd been too fascinated with her surroundings to pay much attention to whom Lyle might have been speaking. She'd just figured it was some discreet servant. But now that she was more focused...this electronic butler thing didn't bode well. She could barely operate an electric can opener. Still, she followed Lyle back into the kitchen. "So, it's a he?" she asked. Lyle glanced questioningly over a shoulder at her. Jayde repeated, "The computer. You called it a he. I was just wondering how...I mean, I know how you can tell if a puppy's male or female. I was just trying to figure out how you'd know on a machine...."

Lyle chuckled. "I get your drift. 'He' has a male voice. And his name is JOCK. J-O-C-K. All capitals. And don't let him fool you—he's the most advanced thing in artificial intelligence there is. Has his own obnoxious personality, too."

With that, Lyle stopped in front of a narrow white wood door set in the wall in the gleaming kitchen and opened it. Jayde thought it must be a pantry. But it was nothing that simple. Instead, mounted on a black panel inside, were enough gadgets and buttons and bells and levers to warm a rocket scientist's heart. Some of them glowed steadily, some of them weren't lit at all and still others were blinking. To Jayde, they all looked ominous.

Her heart thumped fearfully. Surely she wouldn't be expected to know how to operate all this stuff. As Lyle began confidently pushing buttons all over the panel—Jayde was waiting for a missile silo to appear right in the living room—she asked the only intelligent question she could think of. "So, Lyle, what does JOCK stand for?"

Not looking her way, he shrugged his broad shoulders. "I forget. It's computereze for something or other. Okay, here we go." Now he looked at her. "Everything in the house is voice-activated. Once I introduce you to JOCK, he'll obey your every command."

"Really? Will he clean the bathrooms if I tell him to?"

"No. But he'll tell Helga to do it."

"Who's Helga? Another robot?"

"No. The maid. She comes in once a week. You don't have to do any heavy cleaning. Just pick up after yourself, do your own laundry, and keep the kitchen clean."

She nodded and then eyed the control panel, irrationally lowering her voice to a whisper as she leaned toward Lyle. "This JOCK thing won't be, well, watching me all the time, will he?"

Lyle leaned over to her, also whispering. "Yeah, he will. So don't try to steal the silver." Her eyes widened. Lyle chuckled. "I'm just kidding you. But, yeah, there are cameras throughout the house, and JOCK can see you wherever you go. And he hears you through the house-wide intercom system. But it's for your protection more than anything else. You'll get used to it."

Jayde wasn't so sure. But before she could say so, Lyle faced the panel and "spoke" to JOCK, telling it—him—who Jayde was. JOCK welcomed her. "Hiya, toots. What's a cute doll like you doing hanging out with a zero like Lyle? Why don't you step in here with me and I'll show you what a real man is like."

Jayde stood there...dumbfounded. Lyle just

quirked his mouth, crossed his arms over his chest, grinned...and watched her. Like this was a test. Maybe they wanted to see if she'd be rude to visitors. Maybe that was it. So, she went with her good Kentucky manners. "Um, hello, JOCK, nice to meet you. And thank you for saying I'm a...cute doll."

A moment of electronic silence followed. And then—Jayde would have sworn to it in a court of law—JOCK turned to Lyle. "What is she—a virgin?"

Gasping, Jayde blurted out, "I am no such thing. How dare you—" She cut herself off, suddenly remembering that being a virgin wasn't a bad thing.

"Cripes," JOCK said sarcastically. "No need to yell, Jayde. You may speak in a normal tone of voice. I'm not deaf."

Lyle chuckled and good-naturedly smacked Jayde on the shoulder, almost knocking her over. "Come on, Jayde. Don't let him get to you. You got to show him who's the boss, or he'll walk all over you."

Jayde recovered her balance and sought Lyle's gaze, seeking encouragement, which he signaled with a thumbs-up gesture. She then bravely stepped up in front of the control panel. "You might not be deaf, big boy, but if you ever speak to me like that again, you'll be a singing soprano and hitting the high notes in the national anthem." She then turned to Lyle. "I'm sorry. I'll get the hang of this, I'm sure."

Lyle waved away her apology. "You already got the hang of it."

JOCK cut in. "Of course she does, Lyle. After all, *you* did. And you have a single-digit IQ."

Lyle's expression was deadpan. "He's quite the kidder, huh? Yeah, me and JOCK—we're real tight."

After that, Lyle took the time to explain the contraptions on the panel, the functions and workings of each Jayde hadn't a prayer of remembering. In only moments, her head was spinning. Blessedly, Lyle gave her a thick three-ring binder that turned out to be a primer on operating all the gadgets in the house. With that safely tucked against her side, Jayde recapped for Lyle her understanding of the Hale domestic operations.

"Okay, so there's a security system wired directly to the police. A pool service. A yard service. A pest control service. An electronic butler that is voice-activated and runs the whole house. A maintenance man who checks on things once a month. A maid who cleans everything once a week. And no cook, unless Mr. Hale is home for an extended length of time."

"That's right." Lyle's blue eyes were sincere and friendly.

"And Mr. Hale doesn't live here more than a few weeks of the year."

"Yes, Ma'am. When he's here on business."

Jayde nodded. "So, Lyle, what am I doing here? Don't get me wrong. I'm thrilled—if not stunned— to be here. It's beautiful and, I'm beginning to think, a great opportunity for me. But what exactly am I sitting? I mean, this house doesn't need me."

"Sure it does. So does Mr. Hale. See, he likes his homes to be lived in. He doesn't like to think of them sitting dark and empty all the time. He wants someone on the premises who he can call and tell to get things ready when he's coming home."

Jayde frowned, considering Lyle's words. "Gosh, that sounds...I don't know, Lyle...lonely or sad, somehow. As if Mr. Hale is trying to hire himself a family. Does he have one?''

Lyle remained quiet so long that Jayde felt certain she'd spoken out of turn. She lowered her gaze.

''Hey, it's okay,'' Lyle said. ''And no, he hasn't got a family. Not anymore. You know, I hadn't thought about it that way before. Is that how he comes across?''

Jayde shrugged. ''Well, maybe. From what you're saying, it does. But I haven't met him yet. I wouldn't think that someone who had all this would be lonely unless he chose to be.''

Lyle's eyes widened a bit. ''Wow, you've got a lot of insight in that head of yours.'' Then he looked her up and down in a speculative way, adding, ''And potential. It's written all over you.'' Without giving her a chance to ask what he meant, he went on with the business at hand, acquainting her with the surroundings. ''I forgot to tell you. There's a car in the garage you can use anytime you want. Just don't take off for California or anything.''

Jayde could only stare, not believing her good fortune. ''Don't worry. I won't.'' Then, considering her opulent surroundings, she asked, ''What is it—a Rolls-Royce?''

Lyle laughed…but didn't say it wasn't. ''You also have a bank account in your name. Ms. Kingston, back in Kansas City, should have had you sign the signature card.'' Jayde nodded. Lyle continued. ''Good. Your salary and money for household and car expenses will be deposited automatically into the account once a month. And credit cards and a health card will be issued in your name, too.''

Jayde's head was swimming with this sudden embarrassment of riches. All she could think of was how this money—her share of it—would help her family. "Mr. Hale is awfully trusting."

Lyle didn't laugh. "No, he isn't. You've been carefully checked out. Once by the employment agency. And again by Mr. Hale's own security team."

Jayde frowned, feeling very exposed. "That was fast. I didn't even know about this job myself twenty-four hours ago."

"Yeah, they're fast. But you're also squeaky clean."

Jayde stared at him. "That's the second time in twenty-four hours I've been told that, Lyle. I'm beginning to think it's another way of saying I'm boring."

He grinned. "You're anything but boring." Then, he surprised her by adding, "In fact, I'm thinking you're just what the boss ordered—if not what he needs. Imagine…Ms. Kingston sending someone like you." Jayde wanted to ask him what he meant by that, but Lyle was still talking. "I guess you'll find plenty of things to paint here, too."

Jayde stared at him. How did he know that she was an artist?

Before she could get too paranoid, Lyle informed her, "Your artist's easel. I carried it in. And you told me that a shipment of your work is supposed to arrive in a few days."

"Oh, that's right." Relief coursed through her. "I forgot. Whew. For a minute there I was thinking maybe that security check you said Mr. Hale did—"

"Well, that, too. But don't make too much of it. It's standard for anyone who works for Mr. Hale. He just likes to know who he's dealing with."

''Don't we all,'' Jayde quipped, as she wondered what Ms. Kingston had gotten her into.

''WHAT THE HELL—?'' Bradford Hale, newly arrived from Rome, shoved forward from the back seat of his limo, almost joining Lyle in the front as he gripped the leather and stared at his secluded house in the quiet and gated community.

At this moment, though, the entire neighborhood was anything but quiet. Because Brad's home was surrounded by police cars with blue and red lights flashing in the deepening dusk. The courtyard gates were thrown wide and milling officers could be seen inside at the front doors. Security sirens, mounted atop the house, blared. Curious and, no doubt, irate neighbors, none of whom Brad knew, lined their own driveways, gawking at the Hale mansion and talking amongst themselves.

''Looks like something went wrong, Mr. Hale.''

''That would be my guess, Lyle. Just stop here and park. I'm getting out.''

''Yes, Sir.'' Lyle angled the limo over to the curb and brought it to a smooth stop. He cut the engine and pulled an automatic pistol out of his shoulder holster, checking it over. ''I'm right behind you, boss.''

''Be ready, but keep that thing out of sight.'' With that, Brad jumped out and sprinted across the lawns, where he was stopped by a policeman. ''I'm Bradford Hale. That's my house,'' Brad quickly explained. ''What's going on?'' He checked the man's name tag. ''What's happened, Officer Talbot?''

Officer Talbot lowered his arms and had to yell over the sharp wail of the sirens. ''We don't know,

Mr. Hale. We can't get inside to see. Or to turn the alarm off. It's locked down tighter than a chastity belt on a virgin.''

''Damn. I have a new house sitter inside. Is she all right?''

Talbot, a big, burly and competent-appearing man, frowned. ''That would probably be the angry young woman inside, banging on the door, right?''

''I have no idea.'' Brad turned to Lyle, who nodded as he surreptitiously holstered his weapon. Brad again faced the police officer. ''Yes. That's her. Maybe she gave a wrong command to JOCK and he locked the house down.''

''JOCK? That's your security system's computer brain, right?''

''Right. If you'll allow me, I can go undo this. JOCK will respond to me.''

''I sure as heck hope so, Mr. Hale. We're getting complaints here.''

Brad felt his neighbors' accusing glares on his back. ''I'm sure you are. Lead the way, officer.''

Once at the doors, Brad heard the pounding and the yelling on the other side. His expression turned grim. The poor woman had to be scared to death. *That damned JOCK.* The computerized butler was getting too independent. It wasn't employees he was programmed to, well, discourage—it was old and unwelcome lovers, for lack of a better word. Brad decided that, over all, he was becoming a bit concerned by JOCK's behavior. Was the artificial intelligence he possessed getting more real? Was the butler actually thinking on his own? Brad didn't know if he should be excited by or afraid of such a possibility.

Either way, the truth was JOCK's independent actions had already cost Brad two house sitters in the past year by pulling stunts such as this. No sense allowing him to get away with any more games. With Lyle's bulk hiding him from prying eyes, Brad opened a small, artfully hidden panel to one side of the front doors and punched in a few numbers. What he feared he would have to do instead, though, was completely disconnect JOCK once and for all.

"All right," Brad said, closing the panel and turning to Officer Talbot. "JOCK should unlock the door any second now—" A metallic clicking interrupted him. Then the front door swung slowly open.

Immediately, a slender brunette squeezed through the opening and flung herself outside. She looked around, hair wild and her eyes narrowed. She suddenly centered her attention, for whatever reason, on Brad. "I am personally going to kill that damned JOCK. That is the last time he gets around me, you hear me? If it's the last thing I do, I will rip every one of his precious wires right out by the roots. You just see if I don't."

Shocked, Brad stared back at her and then looked over her head to Lyle, who grinned drolly.

"Told you so," Lyle said. "You're wrong about this one, boss. Meet your new house sitter. Mr. Hale, this is Ms. Jayde Greene, lately of Kansas City, Missouri."

THAT EVENING WAS Florida picture-postcard perfect. The police were gone. The neighbors had disappeared. The sun had set beautifully in a manner worthy of applause. And even Lyle, after securing a lobster dinner for two—the two being Brad and his new house sitter—had been given the evening off. That meant Brad was now alone with Ms. Greene, and had been for the past couple of hours.

After she'd settled down, showering and changing into a more weather-appropriate dress, he'd invited her to eat out back with him on the lantern-lit flagstone patio. She'd seemed uncomfortable at first, but the enchanted surroundings, the good food, the wine and hopefully his company had finally worked their magic. She now appeared relaxed as she sat across from him at the wrought-iron table, a gentle wind carrying her perfumed scent his way.

Brad tried his best not to be intoxicated by her, but it was hard. She was an intriguing woman. Attractive. Funny. Articulate. Down-to-earth. And totally oblivious to him. Brad almost chuckled at the realization. No, he didn't want her to come on to him. And no, he didn't think he was irresistible. But he knew that to most people, his money was. Wealth was intoxicating—if you didn't have the onerous responsibility of managing it on your own shoulders, that is. But Brad did and that was why he was determined—with this dinner invitation, this romantic atmosphere, and the wine—to see if he could make Jayde Greene show her true hand, so to speak. If she did, if she came on to him, or made him think she had any ulterior motives at all, then he'd fire her.

Harsh? Yes. But necessary. He needed to know what lay behind her sweet facade and the breath-of-fresh-air personality she had. Quite frankly, even despite her squeaky clean background check, he didn't trust her. If she was a gold digger, then he wanted to know now. Because tomorrow he left for London and wouldn't be back for months. So he had to know tonight if she was trustworthy and simply here for the job, as opposed to being here in the hopes of compromising him and, thus, his fortune. Not that his money was everything to him. It wasn't. But it had proven, with more than one woman, to be everything to each of them. After a few such incidents, he'd become a little hardened, maybe a little jaded. But what else was he supposed to do? Remain a dupe for every opportunistic female out there?

It was no wonder he preferred to trust no one until they proved they could be trusted. Maybe his attitude wasn't fair. If he was wrong, he'd be the first to apologize. But he had every reason to be especially wary of Jayde Greene. Because he couldn't understand why Lucinda would send him someone like her to replace his last house sitter. This woman across the table from him was beautiful and ingenuous. Surely she was a plant, a gotcha, from Lucinda. She had to be. Lucinda Kingston hadn't quite given up on him yet, he knew that much. So it would have made more sense if she'd sent him someone he'd instantly hate, just to make his life miserable. But she hadn't, and Jayde was… well, wonderful. So far. Which could only mean she was probably a partner in crime with Lucinda, someone sent to make him fall hard for her just so she could walk away from him, leaving him face down in the dust. It'd be just like Lucinda, which was why they were no longer engaged.

But was it like Jayde? Was he unfairly prejudiced against her? Well, that's what he didn't know. And that was what he intended to find out. Tonight.

In her favor, Lyle seemed to think she was genuine. And Lyle wasn't easily won over. In fact, Lyle was even more wary of unattached females than Brad was himself. A small smile claimed Brad's mouth. *That damned Lyle*. Brad had often told Lyle that he acted more like a doting nanny than he did a driver and bodyguard. Brad wasn't sure exactly when Lyle had decided that his boss was lonely and needed a wife. Maybe it had started five years ago…Brad shied away from that painful memory. He wasn't going there, any more than he was going to seek a wife among his employees. Not that he needed or wanted a wife anyway.

Brad couldn't stop himself from watching his new house sitter as she stared dreamily at the distant city lights twinkling across the bay. For all the attention she paid him, he could have gotten up thirty minutes ago and gone to bed. She wouldn't have noticed. Brad grinned, employing a bit of self-deprecating humor. Did Jayde Greene think he was boring?

Brad lifted his wineglass and took a sip. Okay, so his new house sitter was, by all signs, totally unimpressed by him. All she'd talked about so far was art and fountains. And all he'd been thinking about as she spoke was how good-looking she was. She didn't have the overtly seductive beauty you'd see on the cover of a magazine. No, she was more the girl-next-door kind of pretty. And she had a nice body to round out the package. But she was more than that. She had something else about her that really appealed to him and, alarmingly, it was getting around all his defenses. Something warm, something earthy and real that he hadn't encountered in many years. Maybe she was everything she appeared to be. It was there in her laughter, in her inquisitive intelligence, in every artless yet seductive gesture she'd made this evening.

Suddenly, Brad realized that he wanted her to be the genuine article, the real thing. He really wanted that. After all his false starts and abrupt endings with women lately, he felt he deserved that. Just then, finally catching the drift of his own thoughts, Brad shifted on the cushioned wrought-iron chair and took himself to task over this apparent dent in his armor of aloofness. He blamed jet lag, the wine, his concern over some business matters, his own loneliness— *Loneliness? Where had that come from? Lyle?*

Brad instantly assured himself that he wasn't lonely. He was a rock. One man unto himself, in charge of his world, a loner. He needed no one. To test that conclusion, Brad looked around himself now, trying to see his property through Jayde's eyes. The manicured and sloping yard before them, complete with banyan trees and majestic palms, gave way to the fine sands and then the azure waters of Sarasota Bay. Moored here at his private dock, and even now bobbing gently in the swells, lay his sleek yacht, a fifty-foot Sea Ray. Pretty impressive stuff. Complete.

He was complete...so let the games begin. He glanced again over at the brunette who still sat in profile to him. She held her wine goblet in her hand. Her expression was serene. And she was essentially and irritatingly ignoring him while he wrestled with his demons. Smooth. Very smooth. Or genuine? Hell, he didn't know. But he did know how to find out. "Still suffering a bit of culture shock, Ms. Greene?"

She turned to him, her doe eyes wide and dark. Oops. Perhaps he'd sounded as put out as he'd thought he had. "I didn't mean to startle you," he said quickly. "I'm just not used to being ignored, especially in my own home."

"Ohmigosh, I'm sorry. I never meant to ignore you. It's just that..." She smiled. "Well, yesterday I was freezing in a blizzard. And now, here I am, basking in Florida sunshine—well, starshine right now—and staring at a yacht. And tonight I had lobster for the first time in my life. So, yes, I have a bad case of culture shock, Mr. Hale.'' Then she grinned. ''Thanks to you.''

Fighting the melting effect of her smile on what he liked to think of as his cool and calculating heart, Brad hoisted his wineglass. ''Here's to no cure for culture shock, then, Ms. Greene.''

''No cure,'' she said spiritedly, clinking her goblet against his and then sipping. As she lowered her glass, she murmured, ''You can call me Jayde, if you like.''

Here we go. The beginning of the intimacies. Brad stared at her over the rim of his wineglass before setting it back on the table. ''Thank you. I will.'' He deliberately didn't reciprocate by inviting her to call him Brad. For one thing, none of his employees, including Lyle, called him by his first name. And for another, he wanted to see what effect it would have on her. From what he could see, it had none. So he upped the stakes. ''That's an unusual name you have, Jayde. But a pretty one. Very pretty.''

And very fake. No one is named Jayde Greene, except maybe in a James Bond movie. That's what he told himself, but to his mounting dismay, Brad secretly liked the way her name, real or not, felt on his tongue. Jayde. Jayde Greene. Surprisingly warm and rich, like a dessert.

''Why, thank you.'' She shot him another one of those killer smiles, one full of openness and trust. Or was it?

Into the ensuing silence between them, punctuated only by gentle sounds of the night, another pang of wanting her and her smile to be real assailed Brad. Maybe his guard was down because he was tired of people being so artificial and cunning, which forced him to be the same way or to be taken every time. And maybe he just wanted to meet one real person in the world, one who didn't give a damn about his money, but who gave every damn about him. What was wrong with that? Or with her being that one?

Just then, as if to further unnerve him, her dark eyes glinted, reflecting the lantern light in such a way that it appeared stars shone in their depths. Brad's breath caught. Was he in danger of falling under her spell, calculated or not?

"You're very kind to say so about my name, Mr. Hale. But I imagine to someone like you it sounds hokey or fake."

Hadn't he just thought that himself? Was this a ploy on her part, or innocent insecurity? The truth was, he was beginning to wonder if, in her case, he would finally be able to tell the difference. "To someone like me? What does that mean?"

Her expression fell. "I didn't mean anything disrespectful."

Brad shook his head. "I know you didn't. It's okay." And it was. Because her comment, as well as her calling him Mr. Hale, reminded him of what he was trying to accomplish here. "And I really do like your name," he added, now purposely flirting with her, trying to draw a suspicious reaction from her. "Although I would at least expect you to have the green eyes to go with it."

"I get that a lot." She looked down at her goblet, her motion causing her mahogany-colored hair to fall forward in a lustrous wave that caught Brad off guard and had him itching to run his fingers through it. But by the time she'd brushed her hair back and looked over at him, he'd picked up his wineglass, sipped at the fine Merlot...and his expression gave away nothing of the man who found himself suddenly and frighteningly yearning for her touch and her laughter, real or not.

"A pretty name was all my folks had to give each of us kids," she added.

Aware of her every nuance, Brad nodded. Not that he understood. He was an only child, one born into a wealth he'd been managing before he'd inherited it outright when his parents had been killed five years ago in an avalanche at a Swiss ski chalet. Since then, he'd worked hard, sparing no one, not even himself, to increase his fortune. Wealth. It was very insulating—none of life's ills could touch you. Or so he'd thought. But lately he hadn't found his life fulfilling—not in the same way he suspected a family of his own would be.

A family, starting with a wife. Well, there was Lyle's influence again. Brad fought a grin and counted himself lucky at least for JOCK's unswerving support and efforts in weeding out the opportunistic females, as Brad called them. "So," he said conversationally...and pointedly, trying to get at any holes in her story, "how many kids are there in your family?"

"Six."

He arched an eyebrow. "Wow. That's a lot nowadays."

"It's a lot every day. Just ask my mother." She chuckled and, before he could stop himself, Brad joined her. Then she continued, "They live in Kentucky. My folks work hard, but there's not a Greene who's ever had much to lay a hand on. But that's okay. Even in those times when there wasn't quite enough food on everybody's plate, we had plenty of love to go around.''

Oh, please. How saccharine. This was too much, this voluntary tale of poverty. True or false, it was not one Brad could relate to, either. But then again, came his sly thought, he wasn't supposed to, was he? She had to know he'd never wanted for anything. He refused to feel guilty about that. Especially when he thought of the boarding schools and the infrequent visits home that had marked his adolescence. His parents had loved him, but they'd kept him at a distance. All of this Lucinda Kingston knew. What a perfect story for her and this Jayde Greene to come up with to tug at his heartstrings. Hell, the Greene family sounded like something out of a Rockwell painting.

''They sound like wonderful people. So, what are their names, these six kids with the pretty names as a legacy?''

He'd be willing to bet she couldn't name them all without stumbling.

But she did. ''Well, there's me. I'm the oldest. And then there're my sisters. Opal, Pearl and Ruby. And my brothers. Garnet and Gem. G-E-M.'' She slanted him a shy, self-conscious glance. ''That's silly, isn't it?''

Yes, it was. And so she had a good memory, so what? Still, he figured if he was going to play the game, he'd best rush in here with reassurances. ''No, not at all. I think it's...'' He searched for a suitable adjective.

"Just too precious, maybe?" Jayde's lips formed a humorous smirk. "Like they're not even real?"

Was she testing him? Brad couldn't believe it. Perhaps she was a lot more cunning than he'd given her credit for. He narrowed his eyes and agreed with her. "Afraid so." Then, capturing her gaze, he heard himself boldly saying, "But let's talk about precious. Precious doesn't have to be a bad thing. I'd bet you're precious to someone."

Shy and beguiling, that was her innocent expression. "No. Just to my family." Then, not looking away from him—not even when sudden awareness sparked in her dark eyes like an electric charge—she all but purred. "But I'd like to be. Someday. To someone. Wouldn't you? Don't you think that's the best thing of all? To have someone to love?"

And there it was. Finally. The playing field was leveled. Something hardened around Brad's heart... before disappointment could clutch at it. She'd just upped the stakes sexually. Brad sobered. He knew how to play this game from here on out. He refused to give in to the surge of emotion between them. Because it wasn't genuine. It was dangerous. Big league. He set his wineglass down on the table, knowing full well what he was getting ready to do. Exactly what Jayde Greene wanted him to do.

He was going to kiss her.

3

JAYDE HAD NO IDEA what to expect when her handsome, worldly employer casually stood up and rounded the table. She thought he meant to refill her wineglass. But no. He gripped the table to her right and the chair arm to her left, effectively capturing her in the middle as he leaned over her. Jayde's breath left her. Her eyes widened, her heart thumped. *He's going to kiss me.* She couldn't believe—

His mouth lowered to hers. He covered her lips, his own warm and firm, hers yielding and hungry. Passion shot through her and all but welded her to her seat. She was powerless to resist the urgency of his mouth, even if she'd wanted to. Which she didn't. She then felt his hand at the back of her head. His fingers slipped through her hair and gently cradled her neck, drawing her up and closer to him. In only an instant, she was on her feet, her hands planted against his chest. He held her to him. Somewhere in her mind, she registered that he smelled fresh and clean and of citrus, like from an expensive cologne.

And his mouth tasted of the wine they'd shared. And his body against hers felt—

He pulled away abruptly, letting her go. Jayde nearly fell forward. He had to catch her and hold her steady. The look on his face, despite its heightened color and his lips being moist with her kiss, suggested that he regretted what he'd done. Instantly uncomfortable, if not slightly insulted—and disappointed—Jayde didn't know what to say, what to do, where to look. Nothing like this had ever happened to her before. She didn't mean the kiss. She wasn't an innocent, by any means. She just…well, she'd never before had a man look so sorry for having kissed her.

"I'm sorry, Jayde," he said, letting go of her and staring into her eyes. His own looked hard…and his words sounded rehearsed. "I had no right to do that. I took advantage of you."

Jayde swallowed, as off balance emotionally as she was physically. She couldn't seem to stop nervously knotting her fingers together. Nor could she catch her breath…or stop the fluttery feeling in her stomach. "I don't feel taken advantage of. I mean…*wow*. That was some kiss. But I am sorry you're sorry. Because I thought it was nice. I did. I liked it. I just—"

"No. I had no right. You're my employee. And as such, you deserve to be treated with the respect due—"

"Whoa." Jayde's raised hand stalled his words. "I already got the speech from Lyle. It's okay."

She was beginning to get mad—from sheer embarrassment. Had her kiss been all that awful? She didn't think so. Still, she did know about sexual harassment, what her rights were, all of that. But this man's kiss hadn't felt as if she was being harassed—not the way it had felt when Mr. Homestead back in Kansas City had tried to catch her alone. Instead, Mr. Hale's touch had seemed warm and real and heartfelt. Until now.

Jayde forced her gaze to capture his and to hold it. She noted again that his eyes were blue. Like the sky. And his hair was a sun-streaked sandy color. Like the

beaches. This man was part and parcel of his surroundings. He belonged here…in ways she believed
she never would. No doubt, that was what was wrong
with him now. The prince had just realized he'd
kissed a peasant girl, who might feel he owed her
something as a result. Disheartened and disillusioned,
Jayde shrugged, affecting a bravado she didn't feel.
"Seriously. It's okay. I'm not going to file a com-
plaint. Or even quit. Unless you want me to, that is."

He shook his head. "I don't want you to quit. But
I really do apologize, Jayde. Sincerely."

She just couldn't take it any more. Putting a hand
on her waist, she quipped, "Well, I wish you
wouldn't keep doing it. I'm beginning to think you
didn't like my kiss." She had no idea where her sudden brashness had come from. The man was, after all,
her employer. And he was one of the wealthiest men
on the planet, which also meant he was probably one
of the most powerful. A man who could have any
woman he chose. A man who—

Realization dawned. That was it. Underneath it all,
he was a man. A warm, living, breathing man with
needs and fears and hopes and dreams. Just like her—
well, except for the fact that she was a woman. Jayde
saw him now as a person, as a man who had kissed
her. He had wanted to, and then he had. Something
about her had stirred him enough to make him get up
and kiss her. What a revelation.

A chuckle escaped Jayde. "You did like it, didn't
you? You liked kissing me. And you don't like that
you did. That's it, isn't it? And now you're afraid—
because of who you are and who I am—that I'm going to want something from you, right? Something
more than my job, I mean. Well, you can rest easy,

Mr. Hale. My job's enough for me. I need this job very much. And I want to stay. So, if you would, please, in the future, keep your hands—and your lips—to yourself, I'll do the same with mine.''

Mr. Hale's blue eyes widened, registering... something. Jayde knew she'd certainly taken him by surprise. Probably no one in his Little Lord of the Manor life had ever talked to him like that. Most likely, he was getting ready to fire her. Well, it wouldn't be the first time, Jayde decided, her sudden bout of bravado leaving her just as Mr. Hale opened his mouth to, no doubt, seal her steadily miserable fate.

But all he said was, ''I'm going to go upstairs now, if you'll excuse me. I think the jet lag and the wine have gone to my head.''

Jet lag? Wine? How about mutual attraction? But no, she didn't suppose he could admit to something like that. How insulting. And demoralizing. ''So I'm not fired?''

His gaze searched hers. Then he shook his head. ''No. You're not fired. Why would you be? You're not the one who did something wrong.''

Great. Feeling cheapened somehow, Jayde still exhaled gratefully. ''Thank you. Well, then, um, good night, Mr. Hale. I'll clean this up. And the kitchen.''

As if he were in a trance, he looked at the remains of their supper...the hollow lobster tails, the empty wine bottle. Then his gaze met hers. ''I'll help you.''

''No.'' Jayde managed a quick and, she feared, wounded smile. ''No. I would prefer to do it by myself. Anyway, I understand this is one of my duties.''

He stood there, nodding, looking trapped by his

own situation. He rubbed tiredly at the back of his neck. "Okay, then. Um, good night."

Jayde didn't move. Like a proud Cinderella, smudged with the ashes of this man's fireplace, she refused to allow him to see her cleaning up after him. "Good night. It was nice to meet you."

"Yeah," he said. "Same here...Ms. Greene."

ABOUT THIRTY minutes after saying good-night, Brad lay in bed, propped up on pillows, his hands behind his head. Overhead, the lazy turning of the fan blades held his wide-awake gaze. The room, with the lights out and the curtains open, was shot through with moonlight. And yet, even in this peaceful setting, in his favorite home, he couldn't sleep. His emotions were a mishmash. One second he was thinking he'd been unfair to Jayde, that she'd taken the blame for everything Lucinda had done to him. Then, he couldn't stop himself from wishing she had followed him up here. If she had, he would have been disappointed in her. On the other hand, he wouldn't be feeling so frustrated right now.

So he lay there...wide awake. And the truth was, he had no more answers than he'd had before their shared dinner. Usually by now, by employing the same calculating instincts he'd honed in his successful business dealings, he would understand a situation. But he didn't. She had him completely bamboozled. Brad exhaled, tired of his own machinations, not liking one bit the adverse ways his innate wariness toward women was affecting him. He tried to tell himself he was overthinking this. Maybe he was so damned jaded—*No pun intended,* he told himself— that he wouldn't know a breath of fresh air if it blew

him down like a tornado. Maybe he needed to let his
guard down and simply enjoy the moment.

As if he had a chance of doing that. Not only was
the memory of Jayde's kiss still frittering his nerve
endings, but so was JOCK and the noise downstairs.
Brad exhaled sharply. Another, though lesser, reason
why he couldn't sleep was because Jayde was still in
the kitchen, arguing with JOCK. From the sounds of
her raised voice and the noise caused by various ap-
pliances whirring, she was giving it all she had...but
was losing badly. But maybe not for long.

Brad heard her voice again, raised in anger. "I said
turn the kitchen lights *on,* JOCK. Not the dishwasher.
The kitchen *lights.* Because I'm standing here in the
dark, that's why, you big bag of bolts. What? Because
I don't *want* the dishwasher on. It's not full. Turn it
off, please. And the lights on." Then she raised her
voice again. "Not all of them at once!" Then there
was a dull thud—and a vile curse, followed by a
threat of physical violence to JOCK's...main mech-
anism.

Dammit.

More enervated than angry, Brad sat up, ripping
the sheet off his legs. Clad only in boxer shorts, he
snatched up a silk pajama bottom and tugged it on.
In another minute or two, he feared JOCK would re-
taliate...no doubt by draining the pool and sounding
a general fire alarm. And they'd be lucky if that was
all he did. No doubt, he'd picked up on Brad's sig-
nals, through his and Jayde's earlier conversations,
that she was an unwanted presence. And now, true to
form and his programming, JOCK was doing everything he could to get rid of her. Again...*dammit.*

Brad tried a light switch. Nothing happened. He

muttered a curse. JOCK had turned all the lights off again. If it was the last thing he did before he left for England, Brad promised himself, it would be to disable JOCK—or at least to reprogram him to be easier to get along with. Now that...well, he couldn't even imagine it. But quickly now, able to see his way courtesy of the moonlight and the wall of windows that faced the water, Brad exited his room and jogged down the circular stairway to the first floor. There was no doubting that he needed to save the house itself from this Jayde-versus-JOCK battle of wills. But there was also no doubting the fact that he just plain wanted to see and interact with Jayde again.

No, Brad argued. He just couldn't let his guard down this quickly. Because it just couldn't be true—Lucinda would not have sent him someone like Jayde without a reason. Lucinda was too jealous and too calculating. Once downstairs, Brad strode purposefully toward the kitchen and he ordered—in a level, no-nonsense voice—"Turn the lights on, JOCK. Now."

The lights came on.

"Thank you, JOCK." Brad's tone lay somewhere between exasperation and sarcasm. And titillation...Jayde was close by.

"You're welcome, Mr. Hale," JOCK replied.... smugly, in Brad's opinion.

Then he rounded the corner into the kitchen. Or what used to be the kitchen. Shock glued him to the spot. But if it hadn't, the sticky goo covering the floor would have done the trick. He couldn't believe the sight that greeted him. The beautiful, gleaming kitchen with its butcher-block island, its hanging copper pots and pans, its restaurant-quality stove, the built-in refrigerator that matched the woodwork. And his lovely house sitter. All of them. Splattered with...food.

Sure enough, there she was, standing across the way...blinking, breathing rapidly, bits of food clinging to her hair. And her dress was caked with, well, cake. In her hand was a wooden spoon, which even now she held up, as if ready to smack at anything that might dart out at her. Far from endearing and genuine, at this moment, anyway, she looked like a cooking experiment gone horribly awry: the creature from the Betty Crocker kitchen.

For long silent moments, Brad couldn't utter a word. He was too afraid he'd laugh out loud. Finally, more under control, he put his hands to his waist, his gaze darting from Jayde to JOCK's control panel. "What in the hell is going on in here?"

"Nothing, Mr. Hale," JOCK said smoothly.

"Everything, Mr. Hale," Jayde shrieked. "Are you aware—" she swiped something sticky out of her eyes "—that this house is possessed? It is. It's possessed. And JOCK is the demon. Go ahead. Ask him what he did."

"JOCK, what are you up to now?"

"You should know, Mr. Hale."

A frisson of guilt shot through Brad. But before JOCK could incriminate them both any further, Jayde advanced on Brad, wooden spoon raised. "What's to know? And he calls this nothing? Look at this place. Look at me. All I tried to do was use the food disposal. And *he*—" she pointed the wooden spoon at JOCK's control panel "and *he* switched it to reverse. All the food came back up. He just threw it up. Everywhere. I mean, I can't believe this, Mr. Hale." She stopped in front of Brad. Her dark eyes were wild, her hair matted. "I don't know what idiot developed and programmed that *thing,* but he ought to be shot and left for dead."

Brad arched his eyebrows...and took his lumps. "I did."

She blinked, finally lowering her spoon. "*You* did? You shot someone and left him for dead?"

"Worse. I developed JOCK and programmed him. I'm the idiot."

"You're the—?" It was as far as she got. Her darting gaze searched Brad's face...no doubt, for sincerity. Then, he could see his words sink in. Jayde slumped, then backed up a step, her gaze running over his face. "Of course you are." Then her eyes widened. "Not an idiot. I didn't mean that. I meant of course you'd be the person who'd create something like JOCK. I mean that in a good way, like wow, you're smart. And creative." She rubbed absently at her forehead. A chipped bit of lobster tail came away on her fingers. She wiped it on her dress. "I should have guessed."

Brad shrugged. "No reason why you should."

"Yeah, right. And I called you an idiot. Great. Boy, there's nothing here not to like, is there? So...allow me." With that, she raised her trusty spoon, giving herself a none-too-gentle whack on the head with it.

Instantly and utterly charmed, despite all his paranoia, by her self-deprecating humor, Brad said, calmly enough, "Ouch. Bet that hurt."

"It did. And it should. I wouldn't blame you if you wanted me to leave."

Not for a million years. For one shocking moment, Brad wasn't sure he hadn't said that out loud. It was bad enough to think it. The thought alone nearly leveled him. He liked her. He really liked her. This was awful…because it gave her great power to really hurt him, if she wasn't who and what she said she was.

Somehow remaining outwardly cool, Brad crossed his arms over his bare chest and calmly looked around his ruined kitchen. Jayde joined him in doing likewise. Then she looked at him. Brad found himself idly noting that she was about half a foot shorter than he was. "I don't want you to leave," he heard himself say…much too sincerely. To lighten the effect of his words, he quipped, "Well, not until we get this kitchen cleaned up, anyway."

IT WAS THE NEXT MORNING. Jayde marveled that Mr. Hale still hadn't asked her to leave. Not after they'd worked hard to clean up the kitchen. Not after they'd again said their awkward good-nights and had separated, heading for their respective bedrooms. And not after he'd had a "reformatting talk" with JOCK about minding her. And not even after he'd packed this morning and had shared with her and Lyle the breakfast Lyle had brought in with him. Coffee, fresh orange juice and a sinful selection of bagels, croissants and muffins.

Seated at the granite-countered breakfast bar that faced the blue waters of the bay, they'd eaten pretty much in silence, except for the occasional and noncommittal comment. Someone said something about the weather. And how nice it was, she'd contributed, to be able to wear shorts in January. Then they'd talked briefly about where Mr. Hale was headed now. London, it turned out. Lyle was going with him. Stuff like that. But then…

"So," Lyle said, as soon as Mr. Hale went upstairs for a suddenly remembered portfolio of some sort. "How are you and the boss getting along?"

Jayde leaned over toward Lyle, keeping her voice as lowered as his was. "Much better than I am with JOCK. He hates me."

Lyle grinned. "He hates everyone. He's got a bad circuit somewhere. I think he ought to be unplugged for good."

"I can hear you both, Jayde and Lyle," JOCK said.

Jayde glared, looking up and around, fully expecting JOCK's embodiment to be either hovering overhead or standing nearby. Lyle sent her a conspirator's grin, which she was pleased to meet with one of her own. She really liked this guy, like she would a brother, and felt she could tell him anything. "He kissed me," she suddenly whispered fiercely.

Lyle's eyes widened. "Who did? JOCK?"

Jayde smacked at Lyle's forearm. "No, Silly. Mr. Hale. He kissed me. Last night. On the patio."

Instantly sober, Lyle sat up, his hands gripping the counter's edge. "Get outta here."

"I almost had to," Jayde assured him. "Not because Mr. Hale kissed me. Well, maybe partly because of that. But more because JOCK threw up and then that little vacuum-thing scooted out of that cabinet down there—you should have told me about that, Lyle—and anyway, it started revving back and forth on its little hose, trying to clean up the mess. And then JOCK—"

"Wait a minute." Lyle gripped her arm. "What are you talking about? Forget the rest and go back to the part about Mr. Hale kissing you."

Jayde shrugged. "All right. But there's not much

to tell. Last evening, right after we'd eaten, he just suddenly got up and kissed me.''

''Son of a—' Lyle ran his fingers over his mouth and chin. Then he focused on Jayde. ''What'd you do?''

''Well, what do you think I did? I kissed him back. And then he apologized and we talked about sexual harassment and how that wasn't what had just happened between us.''

Lyle looked really confused. ''Get outta here. He never.''

''He did so. Ask him.''

Lyle raised his hands up in front of him. ''I don't think so.''

''Since we all know how you don't like to think, Lyle…'' This, of course, came from JOCK.

Again narrowing her eyes—she was just itching for another confrontation with that little eavesdropping electronic busybody—Jayde joined Lyle in staring toward JOCK's dark and gleaming control panel.

''…perhaps you'd like for me,'' JOCK continued, ''to run the videotape back to 10:00 p.m. last night and show you that your employer is indeed capable of lowly human emotions, the most base among them being the need for sexual gratification.''

''Sexual grat—?'' Jayde vaulted off her tall stool. Stiff with indignation, and no small amount of embarrassment, she faced JOCK's control panel. ''Who are you calling lowly and base, you misbegotten hunk of nuts and bolts?'' She couldn't bear to think that she and Mr. Hale had been videotaped last night. Only now did she remember what Lyle had told her yesterday—there were security cameras everywhere.

"Easy now, Ms. Greene. I don't think JOCK meant anything personal—"

"Yes, he did." Jayde rounded on Lyle. "And you butt out. I'll handle this. I don't have five sisters and brothers for nothing." Lyle held his hands up, clearly keeping out of it. Satisfied, Jayde turned on JOCK, pointing an accusing finger at him. "You come out right now, wherever you are, and fight like a man."

"I can hardly do that, now can I, Ms. Greene?"

Jayde wasn't accepting that. "Oh, so you're all talk and no body, huh?"

"It's hard to put anything past you, isn't it, Ms. Greene?"

"That does it." Jayde stomped over to the oblong and evil control panel set flush with the kitchen wall.

"Uh, Ms. Greene, I wouldn't touch anything there, if I were you."

Frustrated in the extreme, Jayde turned to Lyle and gestured wildly. "Well, what am I supposed to do? Just let him have his way?"

"I'm hardly the one you need to worry about," JOCK said, causing Jayde to spin back toward the panel. "But perhaps you might like to put that question to Mr. Hale. I know you felt the sexual tension. I did. The current between you two came close to melting my circuits. And so I believe that was Mr. Hale's intention—to have his way with you. Do you agree, Ms. Greene?"

"Oh, hell," Lyle intoned in the background. "I know what he's doing. I forgot about this. Here we go."

Ignoring Lyle and gasping in outrage, Jayde prepared to sock the smart-aleckness right out of the contraption when someone behind her clapped a heavy hand on her shoulder. A thrill of surreal fear shot through Jayde. Had the electronic voice really taken human shape? Acting on pure instinct, she came around swinging—and clipped Mr. Bradford Hale right on the jaw. The blow knocked him flat to the kitchen floor. He hit hard. The man was out cold.

Following that, the room was deathly quiet. Then… "Ouch," JOCK said. "That had to hurt."

Jayde's shock wore off and horror set in. She clutched at her painful knuckles and then dropped to her knees beside her down-for-the-count boss. Lyle almost beat her there and squatted on Mr. Hale's other side. "Get some water or something," Lyle finally suggested. "Wet a cloth. Cold water."

Jayde jumped up, hurrying to the sink to do as he'd suggested. "Ohmigosh, Lyle, this is so awful. And I am so sorry. He startled me. And, oh, it's just like Kansas City all over again. I can't believe this."

Lyle placed a bar stool cushion under Mr. Hale's head. Then he stared up at her. "What do you mean?"

"Kansas City," Jayde repeated, as if he should just know. Staring wide-eyed back at Lyle, she stood at the kitchen sink and ran cool water over some hastily wadded-up paper towels, which she then tried to un-wad. Not as easy as it looked on TV. "Almost the same thing happened there."

Lyle frowned. "You knocked your boss out there, too?"

Jayde was nearly in tears as she fought the paper towels. "No. I wish. I stabbed him in the belly. But it was an accident. Like this was. I swear it."

"Oh, hell," Lyle said, looking as if he'd just witnessed a UFO landing. "You stabbed your boss in the belly? And here all Mr. Hale was worried about was you might be— Well, Mr. Hale is not going to like this at all.''

''I know,'' Jayde wailed. She hurried back over to her fallen boss and knelt beside him, noting how handsome and angelic he looked, like a sleeping baby...except for the swollen and purplish bruise on his jaw. She couldn't believe it. The mouth that had kissed hers last night so wonderfully well and deeply—and had kept her up most of last night re-membering—now slacked open. The arms that had held her so tenderly last night were now limp on the cool tiles of the kitchen floor.

Worriedly, she rubbed the soggy paper towels across his forehead and over his cheeks. She then focused on Lyle. ''He's going to fire me, isn't he? If he ever comes to, I mean.''

''Don't say that.'' Lyle looked really worried.

''I'm sorry, Lyle.'' Jayde squeezed his hand comfortingly. ''But he is, isn't he? He's going to come to and fire me. And there goes all the painting I wanted to do. And Paris and Rome. And now my family will think I'm a failure for sure. And here I was really starting to like it here. And you, too, Lyle. And him. A lot. I was really starting to like him a lot.''

Lyle's expression became appraising. ''You really do like Mr. Hale.''

It was so absurd, his picking up on that comment, given the present circumstances. She pointed down at her boss. ''Are you serious? Look at him. In the cave days, this would mean we're married. Yes, Lyle. I like him a lot. He's very kind and obviously intelligent. Friendly. And, wow, what a kisser. I like him. But he's going to fire me for sure.''

"Fire you?" Lyle shook his head. "After this, he'll probably make you chief of his personal security team."

Jayde blinked. "But isn't that what you are?"

"Was. Past tense," JOCK said…out of the blue.

Together, as if they'd rehearsed it, Jayde and Lyle turned to JOCK's control panel, and said, "Oh, shut up."

Just then, Mr. Hale stirred, showing signs of waking up. Thus galvanized into relieved action, Jayde helped Lyle handle Mr. Hale's flailing arms. Then Lyle startled her by grabbing her arm, to get her attention. "When he wakes up, let me handle this. He's not going to fire you. I won't let him."

"You're awfully kind, Lyle," Jayde offered, all hope of a secure future having flown. "And I appreciate it. But—"

"No." Lyle's stare intensified, forcing Jayde, who now held one of Bradford Hale's warm hands, to really listen. "Are you sincere and honest in being here, Jayde? Are you who and what you say you are?"

"Well, of course I am. But I don't understand, Lyle."

"You don't need to. But I do. And I'll make it all right, I promise. Just promise you won't leave, no matter what JOCK says."

Jayde frowned. What did JOCK have to do with this? "I promise. But what are you talking about, Lyle?"

"That you're the one for Mr. Hale. He needs you. He doesn't have anybody to complete him. He's too rich and too scared to care. But you can make him. He's been trying to find you for years, only he didn't know it. And now, here you are. And I'm going to fix things. So let me handle it when he wakes up, okay?''

As confused as she was intrigued, Jayde stared at Lyle, not knowing what to think. ''Okay. I guess.''

4

SHE DIDN'T WANT Bradford Hale to leave. It was that simple. She wanted him to stick around and take her in his arms again and kiss her the way he had last night. And she wanted him to keep kissing her…all over. And now that Lyle had planted the idea of the two of them being together into her mind, her body was saying *told you so*…and had been since last night. Hadn't she ached all night for Bradford Hale's touch? For his kiss, the sound of his voice, the feel of his body pressed against hers? It wasn't as if she was easy, either. She wasn't. But she did know what she wanted. And now…he was leaving.

And so Jayde stood at the opened gate to the Hale property and waved goodbye to the occupants of the black stretch limo just now tooling off down the curving road. The pronounced S-shape of the street forced the slinky vehicle to motor slowly past each lushly landscaped yard. Given the dark-tinted windows of the car, Jayde had no idea if her farewell was being acknowledged, or if it was even appreciated.

So, standing there overwhelmed by her yearnings, Jayde put the best face she could on her day. Okay, for one thing, she still had her job. For another, she didn't care if Mr. Hale or Lyle waved back or not—because the two men were now off to Merrie Olde England and that was good, darn it. That meant, number three, that she now had the house and her time all to herself. So, as of this giddy moment—*yippee,* she grimaced—she was officially a house sitter to one of the richest—and one of the handsomest, most aloof—men in the country.

False cheerfulness had never become her. Jayde slumped. The terrible truth was she was here alone, except for JOCK's dubious if not evil company. Lovely. But thanks to the three-ring binder Lyle had given her yesterday, she could handle him and also had a whole list of people to call on if something went hideously wrong with the house. So it wasn't the responsibility of the place, that had her feeling...well, let down, somehow. Or disappointed, maybe—somewhat like she felt on those rare free days when she would be outside in the brilliant sunshine and painting and then suddenly the sun would be obscured by thick clouds and the light would be ruined and she'd have to stop for the day.

That was how she felt right now...as if the sunshine were being driven away in the back seat of the black limo just now disappearing around a bend in the quiet street. Jayde planted her hands on her hips and stood there, a solitary figure in this world of privilege where she would never truly belong. Instant heartache. That's what she was setting herself up for. She needed, right now, this minute, to get over what she was beginning to think of as an infatuation with her boss. The man wasn't some rock star seeking fans. No, she needed to concentrate on what was important to her. Her painting. After all, wasn't it one of the very reasons she'd accepted this position? Yeah, well, that and the threat of imminent starvation.

But still, her feelings for the man ate at her. Witness the giddiness in her belly, and the excitement that fluttered her heart. She couldn't help it. Mr. Bradford Hale's face and laugh and that breathtaking bare chest of his were deeply etched into her female psyche, right beside the remembrance of his kiss. The man was disturbing...in the most delicious of ways. But he was her boss. Her very rich boss. A man who could have any woman, probably including members of royalty, if he so desired. So the last thing she, Jayde Alyssa Greene from Kentucky, needed to have was *very* warm thoughts about her boss. She wasn't in Mr. Hale's league, and she needed to maintain her professional distance.

Well, England ought to be far enough of a distance, she decided as she finally stepped back inside the courtyard, closing the gate behind her and latching it. She turned around—and that was when it struck her. She was really here. In Florida. Standing in shorts and sandals in January in a sensually pleasing and jasmine-draped courtyard. Why, with Lyle and Mr. Hale gone, she could almost make herself believe this was all hers. The car, the money, the house, the pool, the boat. The safety, the security...the happiness. The fountain. With just a short flight of fantasy, she could convince herself that her paintings had financed all this.

Looking around, feeling the sun's rays warm her bare arms, catching the scent of the bay beyond the house and hearing the calls of the gulls, Jayde gave a slow and wondering shake of her head. She'd done it. She'd made her own miracle come true. She was wealthy and successful.

So why was she standing here frowning? Because she knew the truth of her pretty lie. None of this was really hers. She knew that rationally, but her heart wanted to believe otherwise. *No. A big, fat no.* Jayde took herself to task. She couldn't allow her artistic mind-set to delude her rational self. She now glared harshly at her surroundings. All of this—everything that assaulted her senses with a richness beyond money—was, for her personally, only window dressing.

The reality was that her surroundings belonged to Mr. Hale, and the truth was she could be fired at any moment. Hadn't he only just reminded her of that, right before he departed for the airport? Despite Lyle's fast talking and her tearful apology for the bruises on Mr. Hale's face, he'd left no doubt in her mind. If she did one more wrong thing, then all this would slip out from under her.

Now, that stung. Especially because it was JOCK who'd been the instigator of all her accidents. Mr. Hale wasn't being very understanding, Jayde decided. With that revelation went her warm-and-fuzzy feelings for her handsome boss. Forget him and his soul-searing kiss. Good riddance. She was glad he was gone.

In his wake, he'd left her in a mood to paint. The heavy emotions welling up inside Jayde begged for definition, for a true representation in this concrete world. It was at a time like this, when she was reminded of the vagaries of life, of the sheer capriciousness of fortune, that she had to express herself in oils. With bold and bright colors slashed across the canvas. She had a hunger to show the world what she saw in her head. And she had to do it now.

Thus motivated, Jayde sprinted across the warm flagstones of the courtyard, heading for the closed front door. Suddenly, her smile was back. For the first time in her life she could truly indulge her artistic desire whenever the mood struck her. Thanks to Mr. Hale—and Ms. Kingston back in Kansas City—Jayde no longer had to deal with bad weather, the commute to and from work, or long hours of drudgery spent at a dead-end job. She no longer had bills to pay or financial worries of any kind. Nothing stood in her way. She could create to her heart's content. Indulge her talent. Be an original whose work would rock the world of fine art.

She reached for the antique-brass doorknob and turned it. But only her hand turned as she smacked headfirst into the solid wood of the front door. Crying out, with a hand now to her forehead, she tried again. Same results. The knob only jiggled in place. It wouldn't turn.

Realization dawned. The door was locked. And she was locked out. ''JOCK!'' she screamed, beating on the solid wood door with a fist.

''Step away from the door,'' came the stern voice of the diabolically evil butler. ''This residence is armed with an electronic presence that does not recognize your voice,'' JOCK continued. ''I will call the police if you do not cease and desist immediately. Furthermore, the owner of this residence will prosecute all offenders to the fullest extent of the law.''

Jayde wasn't taking this lying down...or locked out. ''JOCK, it's me, and you know it. And I'll be the one to prosecute you to the fullest extent—by cutting off your power supply once and for all, if you don't open this door right now.''

Silence. But JOCK wasn't giving up that easily. ''This computerized system cannot be disconnected from any source outside the residence. Be warned that if this unit should become nonfunctional, nothing inside the residence will operate.''

''Ha. Guess what, Mr. Smarty Circuits? Mr. Hale told me all about this secret panel out here and the code that overrides you. I'm not afraid to use it. And if I do, it will mess up your memory. And Mr. Hale isn't here to reprogram you. That means you'll be out of commission the whole time he's gone. So, it's up to you. Open the door and behave—or say goodnight, Gracie.''

Again, there was silence. Jayde stepped back from the door, waiting. Nothing happened. *Fine.* She reached for the covering to the secret panel.

Instantly, the lock clicked and the door swung slowly open. ''Why, Jayde. Welcome home. Why didn't you just say it was you?''

A BIT LATER that same day, Jayde was out back, standing on the flagstone tiles of the patio and happily painting to her heart's content. She'd been hard at it for two hours, which meant her painting was close to completion. She never bothered with sketching an outline or studying the best angles. No, she felt it was her special blessing that she was able to simply go at it with abandon. Today, she was trying something new. She wasn't painting a fountain. Instead, in an effort to fit into her surroundings, she was capturing the tranquil beauty of Sarasota Bay. But suddenly, something stopped her cold. Her eyes widened. A cold, sinking feeling assailed her.

She hadn't yet informed her family that she no longer lived in Kansas City, Missouri. *Oh...my... God.*

Jayde blinked, focusing again on her canvas...and saw what she'd done. *Oh, lovely.* Her hand had jerked, causing her to fling a sickly pseudoblob of a cloud across the otherwise pristine blue sky. A mild curse escaped her. This was awful—that cloud, as well as her oversight in informing her family. All sorts of dire scenarios leaped into her fertile imagination. *What if they call my apartment, only to hear that my number has been disconnected? Or even worse, they call Homestead Insurance and find out I was fired? No phone and no job equals failure.*

She couldn't allow them to think that, much less to know that was the truth. Jayde took her role as her brothers' and sisters' role model seriously. She hated to disappoint them, but even worse, she hated to worry them. So she had to call them—now. Laying her brush and palette of colors down on the white wrought-iron table to her left, she hurriedly wiped her hands on a rag and tried to remember when exactly she had last called home. Had it really been Christmas Day?

Holy cow. Three weeks ago. She'd never gone more than two weeks without talking to them. Jayde threw down the cloth and headed for the double-wide patio doors, thinking of the kitchen telephone inside.

With each step, she hoped that her news would be a nice surprise. Not a where-have-you-been-we-thought-you-were-dead dressing down. She knew she deserved that, but still, she hoped she hadn't caused her family any worry. But already found guilty in her own mind, with the crime of family neglect, Jayde grimaced as she walked toward the wall-mounted phone and dialed her family's number.

The line only rang once at their end before the

phone was snatched up by Jayde's father. She swallowed. Wasn't that just her luck? With five kids in the house, her father had to pick up the receiver, giving Jayde no time to get her act together.

"Hello, Daddy. It's me," Jayde chirped, fearing she sounded too artificially bright…meaning, guilty.

"Why, Jayde, honey. Hello. Your mother and I were just talking about you, baby. Are you all right?"

"Oh, yes, I'm fine. I just…" She glanced at her watch. Lunchtime here. An hour earlier there. A weekday in both places. Her sisters and brothers would all be in school. That explained why her father answered the phone. Wait. No, it didn't. What was he doing home in the middle of the day? Jayde frowned, forgetting her own news for a moment. "Daddy, is everything okay there?"

A pregnant pause met her question. Finally, he responded, "Oh, sure. It's fine, fine. We'll be okay…if the plant opens back up soon. Don't you worry though, honey. You've got enough on your plate right now."

"Oh, Daddy." Jayde felt like crying. He'd been laid off again. Her poor dad. He tried so hard and nothing ever worked. Jayde rubbed a hand across her forehead and tried to sound as brave as her father was pretending to be. "I'm so sorry. Let me help."

"Now, no." His voice was slow and defeated. "You sent enough money at Christmas. It's my responsibility to see to everyone here. And besides, I hear it gets pretty cold out in Missouri. You'll need to get yourself a better coat than that thin one—"

"But that's just it, Daddy. I'm not in Kansas City anymore." Jayde made a face, wondering when she would be able to stop sounding like Dorothy from *The Wizard of Oz.*

"You're not? Well, where the devil are you?"

"I'm in Florida, Daddy. Sarasota, to be exact."

"Florida? How the heck—Jayde Alyssa Greene, what is going on?"

"Nothing. Well, everything. Daddy, I—"

"Hold on, baby. Your mother wants to know what's going on."

Jayde held on and could hear her father telling her mother in the background that their oldest child had up and gone to Florida. He was saying…well, no, Maxine, he didn't yet know why she would be there, that was what he was trying to find out. Then her mother was saying how she just knew it, that girl has lost her job again—Jayde cringed—and probably run off with some crazy cult or other such nonsense. Jayde rolled her eyes, wondering when they'd remember she was still on the line…the long-distance line.

Then her father answered that he doubted she'd join a cult—and then her mother, ever the practical one, got on the phone. "Jayde, honey, why are you in Florida? Don't I have enough to worry about, what with five other children and your father to look after? Are you trying to worry us to death?"

Jayde had to grin. "No, Mother. I'm not trying to worry you. I'm trying to help you."

"By going to Florida?" Then she yelled at Jayde's father in the background. "Floyd, stir them beans for me, will you?" Then she was back with Jayde. "I've got pinto beans on for supper. Wish you were here to have dinner with us, honey. We miss you."

Jayde's grin mellowed into a poignant smile. "I miss you, too, Mom. And, look, I can help you."

"I wish you'd tell me how. But wait—did I tell you that Gem got hurt in his gym class? Sprained his ankle. But since we never took out that school insurance and doctors are so expensive, Ruby wrapped it up for him. She learned how to do that in her first-aid class. I swear, the things they teach in school nowadays. I just hope nobody in the family *really* gets sick. With the cutbacks at the plant and us about to lose the house, I just don't—"

"Mom? What did you just say?" Jayde interrupted sharply. "Did you say you're about to lose the house?"

There was a moment's silence. Cold dread coiled in Jayde's stomach. "Mama, when did the plant close?"

"About three months ago. We didn't want to worry you, baby. There wasn't anything you could do."

Jayde's chest was so tight she could barely breathe. Her family was about to be tossed out into the cold, when here she was blithely painting away in sunny Florida and living in the lap of luxury. She knew what she had to do. It probably wasn't right, but she had no choice. "Mama, I want you to listen to me. I can help you. I'm—I'm rich now. Really rich."

"What? You're rich?" Her mother called out to Jayde's father. "Floyd, come here. I think the girl has taken a fever." She got back on the line. "You're worrying us to death, Jayde Alyssa. Now what's really going on?"

"I'm not sick, Mother. I just—well, I—"

"You what, baby? You weren't rich three weeks ago? And now you are. What did you do? Run off to Florida and marry some rich man?"

Jayde's eyes widened. It was perfect. And a lie. But

it was also the explanation least likely to get everybody upset. Knowing how traditional her folks' beliefs were, she knew that they'd never accept the kind of money Jayde was getting ready to offer. But they'd accept it from her *husband*. "Yes. I ran off to Florida and married a rich man. Well, not really. I mean, we got married first. And then I moved to Florida, where he has a house."

Her mother let out a whoop of joy, which prompted her father to join in. Jayde knew that their happiness wasn't only because she'd married a rich man—it was because she'd married at all. She never quite understood why her parents thought a woman needed a man to be happy. Jayde grimaced. She'd never met a man who'd made her happy enough to marry him...except apparently the unwitting Bradford Hale.

Jayde recalled her past attempts to bring her folks into the new millennium. Disastrous, that was what they'd been. To get them off her back about being twenty-five-going-on-twenty-six and still single, she'd finally told them the truth. She liked making her own way in the world and she didn't intend to rely on marrying well and retiring from life.

She'd believed that when she'd said it. And she believed it still. But if saying she had married well would get them to accept the financial help they so desperately needed, then so be it. To assuage their pride, maybe she'd tell them that the money she intended to send them was a loan from her and her new husband.

Her new husband. Guilt tore through Jayde. It was as if she could see Mr. Bradford Hale's handsome and smiling face. Actually, she could see it—he *was* smiling back at her...but from the bookcase. A framed picture showed him accepting some award from the President of the United States. ''Forgive me,'' she murmured.

Suddenly she realized that her mother was still talking. ''Did you hear me, baby? I asked how'd you meet him.''

Jayde blinked, coming back to the moment. ''Oh.'' She frowned. ''Um, at an art show. In Kansas City.'' Well, she was certainly in it now—up to her neck. ''He liked my paintings and we started talking. One thing led to another—''

''I don't like the sound of that, young lady.''

''I didn't mean it like that, Mother.''

''You can tell me, baby. I'm your mother. Are you in the family way?''

''Mother! For heaven's sake, I just met Mr. Hale—''

''You call your husband Mr. Hale?''

Her story was already unraveling. ''He's eccentric. The rich are like that.''

''Well, he sounds ancient. How old is he?''

Jayde had no idea, of course. So, in keeping with this whole lying conversation, she made it up. ''He's thirty-four.''

''Oh. Well, that's not so bad. What church did you get married in?''

Here we go. ''Um, it was a chapel. In Las Vegas.'' Jayde warmed up to the idea. ''We flew to Las Vegas and got married. We only arrived in Florida today. That's why I'm calling you now.''

''Jayde Alyssa Greene, I swear—no, wait. That's not your name anymore, is it? What's your husband's name?''

It was getting worse by the minute. What if her mother decided to speak with her new son-in-law?

"Well, like I said, it's Hale. Bradford Hale." And then she declared her independence. "But I'm going by Jayde Greene-Hale in my private life." *Green hail? Dear God.* "I'm keeping Greene because that's my professional name."

"Your professional name? What profession is that, baby?"

The question deflated Jayde. Her mother really didn't know. Her folks had always encouraged her to paint because it made her happy. But she knew they feared she'd die a starved artist. It wasn't that they didn't believe in her. After all, her first attempts at oil painting decorated every room of her parents' home. But their pride aside, they'd still made sure she got a secretarial certificate from community college before she'd left for art school. But given all the lies flying around, maybe it was time to be a world-renowned artist, too. "My painting profession, Mother. I'm going to have my work shown in a gallery here next week. It seems a number of well-connected people in the art world have started taking notice of me."

"Why, Jayde, honey, I don't know what to say. Hold on." She called out to Jayde's father. "Floyd, not only does she have a rich husband but folks actually like her paintings, too." Then she said to Jayde, "Your father is just shaking his head at all this."

He won't be the only one, Jayde told herself. *If Mr. Hale should ever find out about any of this, he'll do more than shake his head. He'll wring my neck.*

THE REMAINDER of the afternoon—following her marriage and the birth of her new career as an artist—proved to be a busy one. There was no rest for the celebrated, Jayde found out soon enough. In her room, after putting away her easel and paints, she'd cleaned up and then reviewed all the papers Lyle had given her. There was her bank card. All she had to do was sign it, his note said. It was already activated. She called the bank...and was stunned at the sum of money at her disposal.

"Is that for a month or a year?" she'd asked, trying not to sound as if she didn't know.

"A month, ma'am, of course," the person on the other end of the line politely answered.

"Of course," Jayde had responded. Then she'd asked for directions to the bank and had found out it was right outside Queen's Harbor. That was easy enough.

And the car keys she had in her hand...*Oh, surely not.* The key ring bore the Jaguar crest. *No, seriously,* she thought. But a peek into the garage revealed a gold Jag...and the keys fit.

From there, the day was exhilarating. There she was...tooling around Longboat Key and Sarasota in a gold Jag with a ready-to-be-mailed money order in her possession. The amount had a comma in it—more money, it seemed to her, than what was in an entire game of Monopoly. In a moment of silliness, she'd penned a note to her folks. *Pay everything up and then come see me.* Not that she ever expected them. Still, she had to admit that would have been fun. She missed them all terribly. And it had felt good to suggest it.

Would it be so awful if they actually showed up? Lyle had said she was allowed to have guests, but only when Mr. Hale wasn't home. That wasn't a problem. Mr. Hale had said he'd be gone for two months.

And her folks—still in this imaginary scenario—
wouldn't stay more than a few days, a week at most.
Their paths wouldn't cross. So...ta-da! But her con-
science wouldn't leave well enough alone. *So, Jayde,
what if they showed up when Mr. Hale was home?
Wouldn't he be surprised to discover he'd hired his
wife?*

Okay, that part was easy. She'd just die. It would
be the only way out.

Using the map of Sarasota which Lyle had put in
her folder of papers, Jayde had no trouble finding the
post office. Moments later, the "loan" and her note
were on their way to her folks.

They'd been very reluctant to accept any money,
especially as large a sum as Jayde had named. But
she'd told them not to worry—it was her money from
her own account. She was free to do with it what she
wanted, and what she wanted, more than anything
was to help her family. Still, they wouldn't let her
send them a dime until she'd agreed to consider it a
loan.

She smiled now. She knew she'd never accept pay-
ment from them, just as she knew they'd never have
an extra dime with which to pay her back. She sighed,
thinking of how pride affected people.

Coming back into Queen's Harbor, Jayde merrily
waved at the guard who promptly raised the bar to
allow her to pass. He saluted her and smiled. *As if I
belong here.* Jayde felt like a queen as she drove past
the fabulously manicured lawns, flower beds and tow-
ering palms, the golf course, the picturesque pond
with a water-spouting fountain at its center—she'd
have to paint it one day—and all the beautiful people
out walking. She continued down the winding streets

that boasted wealth and opulence, the palatial homes and elegant cars and...she turned onto her street, smiling and humming.

My street. She liked the sound of that. She caught sight of her home. Her grin widened. *My home.* She lived here. She belonged. What could be better?

Just then, as the sun was setting on a gloriously sunny day, Jayde slammed on the Jag's brakes and sat there, staring...as her bubble burst and her dream became a nightmare. Gulping, she gripped the polished wood of the steering wheel with both suddenly sweaty hands. With the car's powerful motor purring contentedly right there in the middle of the street, she just stared, her breathing shallow, her heart thumping.

She was a dead woman.

Because, apparently...her husband was home.

5

A FEW FRANTIC moments later, Jayde had left the Jag
in the garage and, not thinking beyond her panic, had
run inside, ignoring Lyle as he waved and drove off.
Suspending common sense, Jayde charged up the spi-
raling stairs. Her sandaled feet slapped against the
long hallway's hardwood flooring. She stormed past
a home theater, a fully equipped gym and an office.
Finally, she swept into Mr. Hale's carpeted bedroom—and stopped cold.

The opulence of the suite of rooms took her breath.
The marble, the tile, the vaulted ceiling, the wood
crown molding, the arched windows with fan tran-
soms, the view of the bay beyond French doors. The
only thing this room lacked were half-dressed men in
turbans to stir the air with peacock-feather fans.

Jayde quickly recovered herself. Putting her hands
on her hips, she spied Bradford Hale in his sheik-
worthy den. There, over by a walk-in closet, which
looked bigger than her folks' living room, stood her
boss. Jayde's heart leaped. His magnificent, though
clothed, back was to her. Looking him up and down,
she exhaled an appreciative breath and tried to remember… What had she run up here to say? Oh,
yes… *Hello. Welcome home. Now, get out.*

But now that she thought about it, she couldn't say
that, could she?

Hardly. Jayde blinked, realizing the man was not aware of her presence, which meant she shouldn't continue to stand here unannounced. Especially since he was steadily shedding his clothes. Jayde swallowed, tempted to retreat. But maybe she was supposed to welcome him home. Hadn't Lyle said something to that effect? So, not knowing what the protocol really was, she cleared her throat and smiled. "Mr. Hale, hello. Um, what are you doing here?"

She watched Bradford Hale jerk around, his hands undoing the knot of the maroon silk tie she'd seen him wearing only this morning. His gaze swept up and down her form. Well, he liked what he saw, that much was evident. Her face warmed with the memory of their kiss last night. But then he spoke, bringing her back to the moment. "I live here, Jayde. Remember?"

That certainly invited comment. "Right. You must be great at whatever it is you do."

A look of surprise, almost of insult, flitted across his features.

Jayde flinched. "I'm sorry. I didn't mean to pry. I just...wondered. I mean, you're so young. But, hey, if what you do is something for which you'd have to kill me because you told me, then, please don't tell me. I am a *firm* believer in the blissfulness of ignorance."

Mr. Hale gave her a considering stare. "It's nothing as earth-shattering as all that," he said quietly. "I'm an investment banker, on an international level. I would have thought that Lucinda Kingston would have told you that much."

Impressions assaulted Jayde. Okay, Lucinda was Ms. Kingston's first name? That was what he called her. So she'd been right—Ms. Kingston and Mr. Hale had something going on...or had *had* something going on at one time. And now he was grim about it. In an effort to match his seriousness, Jayde frowned and nodded. "Well, that's...great. It really is. And no, Ms. Kingston didn't tell me what you do for a living. I guess she thought it was none of my business." She decided to change the subject. "So, Mr. Hale, what happened to England?"

He shrugged. "Nothing. It's still there. But my business isn't. At least, not the meetings I'd set up. Some quasi-political disruption at their end caused them to be postponed."

As he explained his business to her—business that Jayde realized he didn't have to explain to her, since it was essentially none of her business—he pulled his tie through his collar and tossed it onto his large, four-poster bed. He then began tugging his dress shirt out of the waist of his pants. As he did, he eyed Jayde, much as if she were some creature whose next move he couldn't figure out...but had better watch, nevertheless. "Tell me, Jayde, is there some reason why I shouldn't be here now?"

She thought of the huge sum of money—taken from the household account since she wouldn't be paid for another month—and of her note to her folks. Through her guilt, she managed a nonchalant shrug. "No, of course not. I just—" she cast about for something to say. "—I just thought you were supposed to call and tell me you were coming home. So I could get the house ready."

"That's true. I am. But I only left this morning. So, how much preparation time could you need? But, still, I did call and I left you a message. But of course you weren't here, so you didn't get it.''

She rubbed agitatedly at her forehead. ''Well… boy, that'll teach me, huh?''

''No harm done. You're free to come and go as you please.'' He might have said that, but he was also staring intently at her…as if he believed his coming home unexpectedly had, no doubt, put a crimp in her plan to clean the place out.

If only it were that simple. But really, what were the chances of her folks showing up? It was too bad she couldn't call them and tell them to ignore her note. After all, what reason could she give? She or her *husband* didn't want them here? Tell them she'd lied to them? She just couldn't do that to them—or to herself. For once, she wanted something to be good. Only, right now, it was bad…because she'd told lies in order to do a good thing. But then she had another thought. ''So. How long do you think you'll be home this time, Mr. Hale? A day? A night? You probably won't even need to unpack, will you?''

He continued to stare steadily, and unnervingly, at her. ''I'll be staying a while. And unpacking.''

''I see.'' Jayde nodded, smiled shakily. Her heart sank. ''A while? That long? Well, good. That's great. Just great.''

Mercifully, the man stopped undressing. As it was, he stood there in his bare feet, wearing only his dark slacks and his unbuttoned white shirt. He ran a hand through his sun-streaked sandy-colored hair. Jayde's knees nearly gave out. He was so beautiful.

''Where've you been all afternoon, Jayde? Getting to know Sarasota?''

She blinked, thinking that sounded good. "Yes. It's beautiful. Especially around St. Armand's Circle. All those shops. Wow." Then, for some reason, she felt compelled to add, "I stayed away mostly in an effort to stay out of JOCK's hair. If he had any."

A grin tugged at Mr. Hale's mouth...and flirted with Jayde's nerve endings. "Has he been behaving?"

The truth was, he hadn't. But Jayde also knew *he* was listening. And she didn't feel like ratting *him* out, only to suffer some hideously surprising form of retaliation later. So, she clearly and loudly said, "JOCK has been wonderful. We're getting along just fine."

Mr. Hale arched an eyebrow. "That bad, huh?"

Jayde smiled. "I didn't say that. You did."

From there, the conversation seemed to drag. The room seemed to heat up. Either JOCK was playing with the air-conditioning, or being in the same room—the same bedroom—with a semiclad Bradford Hale was causing a tropical heat wave all its own. Jayde didn't know how to leave. And Mr. Hale didn't ask her to go. The moments stretched out.

Finally, Jayde caved, bringing up a sore subject between them—literally. "Um, how's your jaw? It looks like it hurts."

Mr. Hale put his hand to his face, gingerly rubbing the spot where she'd decked him that morning. "It does. That's some right hook you have there."

Remorse ate at her. "I know. It's all those brothers and sisters I have. But again, I'm sorry. I thought you were JOCK, as silly as that seems."

"That's what you said. And like I said, it's okay."

But Jayde couldn't seem to let it go. "Well, you're

very nice to say so. But it's not okay. You probably should have fired me, like you threatened to do this morning. I guess I'm just surprised you didn't.''

His blue-eyed gaze intensified and seriously bored into hers. ''So am I. Anyone else, I would have fired on the spot. And pressed charges.''

''Oh.'' Her mouth went dry. ''Then...why not me?''

For a long moment, he considered her...and then sharply exhaled. ''I don't know. I've been asking myself that all day.''

''Oh,'' Jayde said again. Then it got really quiet between them. Again, she caved first. ''Well, I'll just—''

''Why don't you—'' he said at the same time.

''I'm sorry. What?''

''No, you first. What were you going to say?''

''I wasn't. I was just...'' She gestured vaguely toward the open doorway to the hall behind her, indicating she'd thought to leave.

''Oh. Okay. Sure,'' he said. ''Go ahead. And I'll...'' He gestured just as vaguely behind himself toward his walk-in closet.

She got his drift. He meant to continue changing his clothes. But still Jayde stood there, as lost in her embarrassment as he appeared to be in his.

''So, good. That's settled,'' she said a bit too loudly. ''I'll just go downstairs and let you...'' She wagged her hand at him, meaning he should carry on. ''I'll be downstairs...if you need my help.'' She suddenly heard how that sounded. ''I meant if you need *me*.''

Okay, that was worse.

NEED HER. Grinning, Brad pulled on his khaki shorts and then reached for a white knit golf shirt. He couldn't get over how seeing Jayde in his bedroom had affected him, however innocent her presence had been. He thought about her again, looking to where she'd stood only a moment ago. It was as if he could see her there. Her dark hair swirling around her shoulders. Her even darker eyes wide. Her slender arms and legs. The way she looked in her shorts and T-shirt. She'd be magnificent on the deck of a yacht at sea. Or better yet, in his bed. He took a moment to fantasize about that before he beached his thoughts on solid ground. He remembered how her face had turned red with her last words. Then she'd fled, as if he'd been chasing her.

He hadn't been, of course. Brad quirked his mouth, thinking maybe he should have. He sure as hell wanted to. Okay, what if he had? It was like when a dog chased a car. He'd always wondered what a mutt would do with one if he caught it. Not that Brad didn't know what to do with a woman, but the point was…he hadn't chased Jayde because he still didn't know if he could trust her. But even if he did trust her implicitly, would she want him to chase her? He didn't know.

So, right now, she was downstairs. Where she belonged. His expression severe, he reminded himself that she was his employee. And there was no playing around in that pool. That was his rule. And a good one, it was. Nothing got messy that way.

Except maybe his entire house. Brad sighed. How well aware he was that she was downstairs—and not only from her magnetic pull on him. As he buttoned up his shirt, he could hear her fussing with JOCK. He braced himself for the electronic butler's retaliation. Sure enough, and right on cue, as if Brad had signaled it, an Italian tenor burst through the argument to perform, at an ear-piercing level, an angst-ridden solo over the built-in music system. Brad's eyes began to water. He shook his head and gave up trying to corral his wayward emotions where Jayde was concerned. Instead, he thought to save his—and her—eardrums.

He stalked over to a control panel in his room and punched the volume control button until the tenor's powerful voice was reduced to a pathetic warble. "Knock it off, JOCK," Brad warned aloud. He then waited. Nothing happened—meaning, no further rebellion on JOCK's part. Brad shook his head, fighting a grin. The hell of it was, through it all, including messes and noise, he liked knowing Jayde Greene was downstairs. And he liked being home here with her, just the two of them. Well, the four of them, counting JOCK and Pavarotti.

So what if his meetings—important meetings—in England hadn't been canceled by any disruptions over there? He'd canceled them himself. What's more, he'd done so because, dammit, he needed to know the truth about this Jayde Greene. He also just wanted to spend some time here in Florida. He'd told Lyle he was tired and the business meetings could wait. But that damned Lyle had been unbearable—grinning and winking—as he'd driven Brad home.

Brad couldn't believe this. What was happening to him? He ran a hand over his mouth and turned his back on his full-length reflection in the mirror behind him. He knew that if he looked, he wouldn't like what he saw. A lonely man acting like a love-struck high school kid. One who didn't care if Jayde turned out to be the biggest gold digger on the face of the planet. So what if she was? He wanted her—

Brad's knees stiffened. Why did Jayde have this effect on him? He felt raw and edgy and restless. Why? Because he was attracted to her. Strongly. Fatally. Even worse, he felt that he was supposed to hold her and kiss her forever.

For some reason, he thought of his other house sitters. Well, maybe not the family butler, the thousand-year-old Crittenden, who held down the Kansas City fort, as Brad thought of the Hale property there. But the house sitters at his villa in Rome and the chateau outside Paris. They'd never affected him like this. Okay, so those dear women were grandmotherly—Brad caught himself. He looked around. Why was he standing here thinking about all this? He took in the opulence, the richness, the beauty of his surroundings. And looked right through it all, for the first time. It no longer satisfied him. It no longer insulated him against his life alone.

Brad put a hand to his temple and rubbed, wondering what the hell was wrong with him. He had friends. He had a social life and women he kept company with. And there it was again—his original conclusion.

None of them was Jayde Greene. The inescapable truth was, he felt as if he'd known her all his life. He'd never felt that way about anyone before. Not even Lucinda Kingston, whom he had actually known all his life. And whom he'd come damned close to marrying recently...until he'd finally realized she loved his money a lot more than she did him. What an ugly breakup that had been. He could still hear her saying she'd get even with him for embarrassing her by canceling their wedding last spring. As a gesture of goodwill and in an effort to smooth ruffled feathers, he'd told her he'd still use her agency—and continue to pay her handsome fees—when he needed an employee. And here Jayde was, a first test of that gesture of his that, he was now willing to admit, was really more of a payoff to Lucinda than goodwill.

And how had she, Lucinda, repaid his generosity? Oh, by getting even with him, just as she'd said. But now he realized—and what a revelation it was—that there was no devious plot between Lucinda and Jayde. No, he'd just bet that Lucinda believed that she'd done him a worse turn by sending him an innocent. Because Lucinda knew that he hated incompetence, that it drove him mad. And so she'd sent Jayde. Unbelievable. It was now so obvious.

Jayde was truly in over her head here, what with the technology and the responsibilities of the place. In some respects, it was akin to running a private resort. But all that aside, she'd riled JOCK to the point of Brad's having to reformat the butler. She'd punched him in the jaw. And she'd gotten herself locked out. She'd even won Lyle over. And now, all he—Brad—could do was stand here laughing at her antics, which he should be terming offenses. She should already be gone. And yet, she wasn't.

So why wasn't she? Well, for one thing, Brad reflected as he rubbed his sore jaw, damn it, he respected her because JOCK hadn't been able—yet—to send her packing. Brad liked Jayde because JOCK had met his match in her. And to Brad that meant that he, as JOCK's creator, had met his, too. An interesting concept, Brad decided, continuing to rub his chin. And an exciting one, too, if his body's reaction to her nearness was any indicator. Wouldn't Lucinda be surprised when he sent her a thank-you note for finding such a jewel—pun intended—as Jayde Greene?

Brad almost laughed out loud as he tried to picture Lucinda's face. No doubt, she expected him to already be on the phone, giving her hell…to her delight. Good old Lucinda. Brad shook his head. He didn't hate her, in fact, he didn't even dislike her. She couldn't help how she was…any more than he could help how he felt…about Jayde.

Suddenly Brad realized that he had a lot to make up for. She had no idea of the dark things he'd suspected her of, and he wasn't about to go apologizing. But he was going to be nicer. A lot nicer. His masculine hormones kicked in, reassuring him that he was on the right track now. And that felt good.

Well, there it was. Grinning, wanting to relish this good feeling for just a moment more before he joined the fray downstairs, Brad strolled over to the French doors across the room from his bed. He threw them open. A gentle breeze, still warm even though this was January, caressed his body. Further heartened by the bloodred colors of the setting sun, he stepped out onto the balcony and gripped the railing. He looked out over the bay, which glittered as if it were awash with sparkling jewels. Then, Brad actually felt, for the first time, deep inside himself, the calm and the beauty of the sunset. It was amazing.

Just then, a movement below caught his eye. Brad focused on the flagstone patio below him. His heart tripped. There, by the wet bar, Jayde was wiping off the wrought-iron table. Brad knew it was wrong to watch her while she was unaware. But he couldn't stop himself. As she leaned over the table, she was, to him, more mesmerizing than the setting sun. Her swiping motions moved her body as if she were engaged in some sensuous dance, as if she moved to music only she could hear.

She was magic. A breath of fresh air in a stale world.

Without warning, as if she had sensed his attention, she looked up. Brad froze in place, even as she did a double take, her gaze finally locking with his. She tossed the wet cloth onto the tabletop and blatantly stared up at him. A smile spread across her generous mouth. Affected as he'd never been before in his life, Brad leaned over the smooth masonry of the balcony railing, settling his crossed arms atop the sun-warmed stone baluster in front of him.

"How perfect is this, Mr. Hale?" she called. "If you were down here and I was up there—and if I knew the lines—I'd be reciting from *Romeo and Juliet*."

Brad chuckled. "Oh, go ahead. Try."

She shrugged. "All right. You're the boss." Melodramatically clasping her hands together over her chest, Jayde plaintively cried, "Oh, Romeo, Romeo, wherefore art thou, Ro—" She dropped the pose. "No, wait. I'm down here, so I'm Romeo and I'd know where I was. And you're up there on the balcony. So that makes you Juliet, right?"

"Not unless she needs to shave her legs," Brad quipped, feeling lighthearted for the first time in a long time.

"I wouldn't know. But still, you *are* the one on the balcony."

He couldn't argue with that. "You got me there. Okay, I'll give it a try." He cleared his throat and called out, ''Oh, Romeo, Romeo—' He looked down at her. Her hands were clamped over her mouth and her shoulders were shaking. She was laughing at him—at *him*, international investment banker extraordinaire. Fighting a grin, Brad called down, ''I can't say that. I'm a guy.''

She looked up at him. ''Well, thank God. That explains the hairy chest.''

Brad couldn't help laughing. And knew they'd just crossed some line. He wondered if she felt it, too— the tug between them. The sharp awareness. All he knew was she made him feel as if he could simply hop over this balcony, jump to the ground, and take her in his arms. He couldn't seem to help himself. It was as if they'd gone to that place where their bodies, and maybe their souls, communicated with each other on some unconscious level. It was the oddest thing. And, yes, a little frightening to someone who'd never felt it before.

Brad didn't want to move, lest he break the spell between them. Then the doorbell rang—but not like any doorbell Jayde had ever heard. Brad's eyes widened. So did Jayde's.

''What's that?'' she called up to him, sounding a little shrill.

Brad didn't blame her a bit, given all of JOCK's antics of late. ''I think it's just the doorbell. But I couldn't swear to it because I'm not sure I've ever heard that sound before.'' Then, just to tease her a bit, he looked down at her and grinned. ''Are you expecting company?''

AM I EXPECTING COMPANY? Jayde felt certain she was drowning in a big pool of guilty sweat as she stood there staring up at her boss. Logic told her it just couldn't be. She'd only just mailed the money and the note to her parents a matter of hours ago. Her letter probably hadn't even left Sarasota yet. So it couldn't be her folks. Finally, she managed to shake her head. "Me? Expecting company? No. Of course not. I don't know anybody here. Except you and Lyle." She latched on to that. "That's it. It's Lyle. He's bringing supper, right?"

Mr. Hale shook his head. "No. I told him we could fend for ourselves. He's got the night off."

She spread her hands wide. "Then I don't know."

"And yet, I do." JOCK's voice came from the speaker mounted in the outside wall, right below the security camera. "Ask me."

"All right, JOCK," Mr. Hale said, an eyebrow raising as he nonetheless continued to stare down at Jayde, who was beginning to feel like a butterfly pinned to a display. "Who's at the door?"

"A delivery person."

Delivery person. Relief coursed through Jayde. *Oh, thank you.* She resumed breathing.

"What's he delivering?" Mr. Hale asked.

"Not he," JOCK informed his creator. "She, Mr. Hale. Two shes, as a matter of politically correct fact. And a rectangular package, to answer your question—one secured in a large and apparently heavy cardboard box. Shall I answer the door? I believe the delivery persons, apparently being of the impatient sort, are going to ring the bell—"

The bell rang again.

"Well?" That was JOCK.

"Tell them I'll be right there," Mr. Hale informed his butler.

''As you wish,'' JOCK said, signing off.

Mr. Hale looked down at her. ''Would you mind, Jayde? You're closer. And I'll be right behind you, even though I'm not expecting anything.''

''Oh. Sure.'' She set off in motion, heading for the sliding-glass doors that led into the elegant breakfast nook. What in the world could they be getting that was wrapped up in a large, rectangular box? If Mr. Hale wasn't expecting anything, then certainly she—

Ohmigosh! My paintings!

She remembered now. She'd had to ship them. How could she have forgotten something so important to her? Excitedly, she crossed the kitchen, rounded the corner, skirted the devastatingly formal dining room and finally made her way to the crystal-chandeliered gallery entryway when Mr. Hale came bounding down the circular sweep of the wide stairway. True to his word, he was right behind her.

She grinned at him as a part of her brain noted the virile handsomeness of his straight nose and high cheekbones, the deep set of his blue eyes, the tug of his masculinity on her...well, femininity. ''I know what this is,'' she told him excitedly. ''It's my paintings.''

He frowned as he reached around her for the door-knob, his closeness all but pinning her between his body and the wall. ''Your paintings? I don't get it. What do you mean?''

Her heart beat happily at his being so near. ''I mean mine. The kind I painted.''

He evidently forgot the doorknob in his hand. ''*You* painted? You're an artist?''

''Well, not of the caliber you have in your home. But I hope, one day, to rival them.''

He let go of the doorknob, obviously quite taken with this turn of events. "No kidding?" He put his hands to his waist, adopting a conversational pose. "That's really great, Jayde. I never guessed I had such a beautiful accomplished woman right here in my own home."

Jayde absolutely preened under such compliments. She didn't dare touch the "beautiful" comment. But the other... "Well, I don't know if I'd go so far as to say 'accomplished,' Mr. Hale. I just dabble. Really, I—"

"Excuse me?" JOCK interrupted. And he sounded bored. "Might I break in to ask that one of you answer the door, please?"

6

BRAD SAT at the round oak table in the breakfast nook and stared at the paintings Jayde was proudly propping up around the room. When she finished, every surface held a picture she'd painted. She now stood to one side, across the room from him, her hands clasped in front of her. She had her bottom lip gripped between her teeth. Her eyes were wide and she wasn't blinking. She was, however, staring at him, waiting expectantly for his comments.

Brad pushed his chair back from the table and sat forward, bracing his elbows on his knees and covering his mouth with his steepled fingers. He allowed his gaze to again sweep the body of her work. He fought to keep his expression neutral, but his underarms felt sweaty…and he wished like hell he'd gone on to England.

The paintings were awful. Indiscernible of subject matter. Unfathomable in intent. Painful. If she'd turned them all upside down, he wouldn't have been able to tell the difference. Almost against his will, he met Jayde's stare.

''Well?'' she chirped, her voice proud and hopeful. ''What do you think? I realize—just from examining the pictures you own—that you've got a good eye for art. And I know I'm not in a league with the Picassos or Rembrandts of the world. But do you see anything in these at all? How do they make you feel?''

Like he had a hangover, actually. The thick, goopy strokes she'd applied to each canvas hurt his eyes. He felt the beginning of a headache…and he didn't get headaches. Even JOCK was struck dumb. The electronic butler had taken one ''look'' and had actually turned himself off. *Damned coward,* was Brad's assessment—of JOCK and of himself. With that, he sat up and faced his house sitter. ''Well, Jayde, I—''

''Wait.'' She stared at him, her eyes bright. With unshed tears?

Had he waited too long to speak? If those were tears in her eyes, he'd—

''I just want to say something before you give me your opinion, okay?''

Relief at not yet having to render that opinion had him gesturing his heartfelt encouragement. ''Please.''

She slumped, as if with relief. ''Thanks.'' She spared a glance for the painting closest to her and reached out, lovingly touching it. Then she again focused on him. ''You know how you have a talent for making money?''

That took him by surprise. He hadn't before thought of his business acumen for amassing a fortune as a talent, not in the creative sense, anyway. But for the sake of the discussion, he said, ''Okay. Yes.''

''Right. Well, I believe that each of us is born with a special gift. A gift that defines us and never lets us down. Like you, for example. You have a talent for producing wealth. And that's good. Very good. The world needs that. But I can tell you're also good at everything else you do, too. You're just that type of person.''

Brad was really getting uncomfortable. "Jayde, I don't know where you're going with this, but I—"

"Please, Mr. Hale." She held out a hand to him. "Let me finish. Now me, I'm different from most. See, I'm not really good at anything. As you've seen, I mess everything up. And I'm accident-prone—only I hurt other people, like you, for instance. I mean well, but I can't even keep myself from getting locked out of your house. Or manage a butler who's just a bunch of wires and circuits."

"Don't be so hard on yourself. He's done the same thing to me."

Jayde smiled…as if she didn't believe him. "Maybe. But what I'm getting at is—" she swept her arm out, indicating her paintings "—*this* I can do. I can paint. I may lose all my jobs—even this one some day. And that's okay. Well, it's not. I mean I don't like being incompetent—"

"You're not incompetent." It surprised Brad how angry he got hearing her essentially putting herself down.

Again she smiled. "You're just being nice."

"No. I'm not. I'm not known for being nice."

Jayde frowned. "Well, I think you are."

Brad looked away from her, away from her awful paintings, away from her need for his approval. His chest felt constricted. He focused on the dying day outside. The sky had gone from streaks of red and rose to shades of gray and black. Why did this have to happen now, when he'd just discovered he could be himself around her? Why?

"Anyway," Jayde blurted, regaining his attention. "Being able to paint is what keeps me going. In fact, the main reason I took this job was so I'd have the time to develop my talent. One day, I might even be able to make a living at it. I might even be as successful as you are."

Brad stared into the darkest, most sincere eyes he'd ever seen. A silence spread out between them. Then, Jayde gestured abruptly. "That's all. I just felt it was important that you know I have ambitions and drive, things like that." Then she gave him a slightly stricken smile that begged him to be gentle. "So, what do you think?"

As he looked at her, she crossed her arms. Brad was an expert in body language. He had to be, in his business. And he recognized the classically defensive—and in her case, defenseless—posture. In that instant, unfamiliar emotions assaulted his senses. Compassion. Protectiveness. Tenderness. Dammit, a genuine caring about the feelings of another human being. He'd never allowed these weak-kneed emotions to get a grip on him before. They had no place in his world of cutthroat finance.

Every day he fought a bloodless war with numbers, with people who knew the rules. Even the women in his life had known the rules. But Jayde Greene was different. She was real. And she was an innocent. Brad looked her up and down. Suddenly, his heart lurched and he realized he was smiling.

"I love them," he heard himself saying.

"YOU'RE LYING," Jayde said. Hurt, and not really knowing why, she began gathering up her paintings. Banging them together carelessly, she piled the canvases against the tiles of the breakfast bar. "You hate them."

"I do not," Mr. Hale protested, suddenly on his

feet and trying to tug from her grasp her rendering of a particularly ornate Kansas City fountain. He won the battle. "Like this one." He now held up the picture at eye level. "It's beautiful. Very evocative."

Jayde arched an eyebrow and crossed her arms. "Of what?"

Mr. Hale lowered the canvas. "What?"

Jayde pointed to the painting in his hands. "You said it's evocative. I'm asking you what it's evocative of."

He looked again at the painting in his hands, then at her. His expression was that of a man who'd just been told that his very life depended on him correctly, in the next five seconds, coming up with the square root of 757,281.

"By the way, you're holding it sideways."

He cut his gaze down to the canvas in his hands and then promptly turned it. "I was holding it like that for added perspective."

Jayde sighed. "Then turn it the other way. It's still wrong."

He turned it the other way. And smiled. "There. Oh, okay. Now, I see. It's really beautiful, Jayde. I love it. I do."

She didn't say anything.

Very carefully, as if it were stained glass, Mr. Hale put the picture down with the others and turned to her. He ran a hand through his sandy-colored hair. "Your first time to show your work to anyone?"

Completely demoralized, she nodded. "Yes. Well, outside my family, anyway. And who can believe family? They have to love everything you do."

He nodded. "I wouldn't know about that. But you're just feeling what every young artist does."

Jayde stared wide-eyed at him. "You called me an artist. You're the first person to do that. So, you really think that I'm just, well, unduly neurotic, like I'm supposed to be?"

"Yeah, I do." He sounded as excited as she did. Then he sobered. "Well, not neurotic. You know what I mean."

Jayde watched him. Besides being so darned handsome, Mr. Hale appeared sincere. Which only made her feel worse for feeling mean toward him. Maybe he was right. Maybe it was because he was the first person, other than her family, that she'd ever shown her paintings to. And maybe it was because she wanted—needed—so desperately to believe him. It was just…to see the work of her soul so exposed. Well, it made her feel vulnerable. Her worst fear was, what if it turned out she really wasn't even any good at painting? She'd have no dream left.

Suddenly she realized Mr. Hale was watching her. "Are you all right, Jayde? You look scared."

"Oh. No. I'm fine," she blurted, attempting a smile. "I guess it's that whole eye-of-the-beholder thing, right? Isn't that what you're really saying?"

He smiled. "Exactly. You know, some people don't even like the *Mona Lisa*. Art is a matter of taste. But who am I to tell you that? You're the artist here."

She winced, unable yet to believe him. "Maybe."

He narrowed his eyes. "All right, you still need convincing. Look around you, Jayde. Everything in this house shows *my* taste. What do you think of it?"

She suddenly felt too warm—as if she were about to flunk a very important test. Her chin quivered, but she humored him, looking around, taking in the rich appointments of what had to be a three- to four-million-dollar home. Finally, she shrugged. "What do I think? I think it's fine."

Mr. Hale chuckled. "Oh, please. Your praise is too much."

Jayde smiled. "No, seriously. I mean it. It's fine. It's fabulous. I love everything here. It's gorgeous and tasteful and elegant. Really."

"You're lying. You hate it." His inflection was flat, deadpan.

Frustrated, Jayde shook her head, started to protest—and then realized what he was doing. She wagged a finger at him. "Oh, I get it. It truly is beautiful here…the decor, the furnishings, everything. *But* if you were insecure about your taste, you wouldn't believe even an honest assessment. Right?"

Mr. Hale crossed his arms over his chest and grinned. "Right. And no matter how many people told me otherwise, I'm not sure I'd ever really believe they were being sincere. Even if I attained great success, I'd probably fear every new person's opinion."

Now Jayde really had to struggle not to cry. Mr. Hale was just so wonderfully kind. "Wow. You know your artistic types, don't you?"

He shrugged. "I've been around a few."

Finally, she gave in. "You're very kind, Mr. Hale."

"Well, don't let it get around. It could cost me a lot of money." Then, his blue eyes glinted, warming—in Jayde's opinion—to the aquamarine of Sarasota's noonday waters. "And why don't you call me Brad?"

Jayde blinked in surprise. "Well, because Lyle told me not to. He was very clear on that."

Mr. Hale frowned. "No. You misunderstand. I

didn't ask you why you don't. Well, I guess I did. But what I meant was why don't you. As in, I'd like for you to do so.''

Jayde shook her head. ''I couldn't. If Lyle found out—''

''Lyle isn't your boss. I am.''

''I know that, but—'' She looked around furtively and then stepped closer to him and whispered, ''Lyle carries a gun. Did you know that? I saw it under his coat this morning. It's in one of those shoulder-holster things. I wouldn't want to make him mad.''

Silence met her revelation. Her gaze locked with his. Then Mr. Hale rubbed at his forehead...rubbed hard. He exhaled. ''I know he carries a gun. It's part of his job as my bodyguard. But it's none of his concern if I ask you to call me by my first name.''

Jayde swallowed. ''Okay...I guess.'' She gathered her courage and gave it a try. ''Brad.'' She waited, cringing. But when nothing happened, she felt emboldened. ''Hey. Cool.'' She said it again. ''Brad.'' Still nothing horrid happened. ''Brad.''

Brad held up his hands. ''Okay. You've got the hang of it now. Look, why don't we have a drink and see what we can scare up for supper? And then, with your permission, I'd like to display some of your paintings in the living room.''

''Why?''

''I'd like for Lyle to see them tomorrow. You know, get his opinion, too.''

That fear born of insecurity flared and must have shown on her face because Bradford Hale held up his hand. ''Hey, the more opinions you get, the more used you'll be to people having their own opinions about your work, good or bad.''

She backed up. "I don't want more opinions… Brad. I'm not ready. Especially not for Lyle's. My work might not be to his taste and he'd shoot me."

Brad's expression became encouraging. "Oh, come on. You don't really believe that, do you? Lyle's a teddy bear."

Brad took a step toward her and her heart picked up its pace. He was so close Jayde could see how long his eyelashes were. "Well, maybe you're right," she said quickly, not really knowing where to look. She settled for a button on his knit shirt. "He's been nothing but kind."

"That's more like it," Brad said, drawing her attention up to his face. He was so good-looking, Jayde felt weak in the knees and her mouth went dry. Brad didn't seem to notice her nervousness as he gestured toward the stack of canvases leaning against the breakfast bar. "You know, Jayde, you have enough paintings here to have a gallery showing of your own."

Jayde's heart hammered—with fear. She stepped back and flitted around Brad, rushing to gather up her work. "No, no, no. No gallery showings. Besides, quantity isn't quality. It was hard enough showing them to you. Besides that, it would make me sick. And maybe a lot of other people, too."

IT WAS TWO DAYS LATER and Brad still could not say why he was pushing Jayde so hard to have a gallery showing.

"Wow. Nice shot, boss," Lyle said, commenting on Brad's drive from the eighteenth tee of the private Longboat Key Golf Course.

"Thanks," Brad acknowledged, squinting behind

his sunglasses as he watched his ball sail high and cleanly down the middle of the fairway. He then handed his driver to Lyle, who today was playing caddy.

Lyle took the club and trudged along behind him, back to the golf cart. "It's been good for you to take some time off, boss. Your game's improving."

"Thanks," Brad said absently. As he climbed into the cart and waited for Lyle to stow the club back in the golf bag, Brad found himself wondering what Jayde was doing. He had the feeling she was avoiding him. Maybe he'd been too familiar, too fast. He shouldn't have been familiar at all, was more like it. In fact, he should be glad she was keeping her professional distance.

Still, he wouldn't have thought that two people could be in the same house and not run into each other. Even in a house the size of his.

"You okay, boss?"

Brad blinked back to the moment. Seated on the driver's side of the cart with his arms draped over the steering wheel, Lyle waited for a reply. Brad exhaled. "I'm fine, thanks."

"That all you can say? Thanks?"

"What do you mean?"

"For about the past hour, you've answered all my questions with 'thanks.' You thinking about her again?"

Despite feeling his face heat up, Brad adopted a stern expression...and played dumb. "Who, Lyle?"

Lyle stared at him, then grinned and straightened up, setting the cart in motion as they headed farther up the hilly course. "Okay. Have it your way."

Brad glanced over at his chauffeur-bodyguard-caddy. "I'm not thinking about her."

Lyle chuckled. "Whatever you say."

Brad glared off to his right, taking in his beautiful surroundings. The swaying palms. The blue waters of the bay. The white sand of the traps. The red of the flowering hibiscus that dotted the course. He turned back to Lyle. "You know she's an artist, don't you?"

Lyle nodded. "You said as much. She any good?"

Brad shook his head. "Awful."

Lyle exhaled. "That's not good."

"No. But, stupidly, I tried to talk her into a gallery showing."

They drove along for a few seconds, both staring ahead. Then, into the silence, Lyle asked, "Why'd you do that?"

Brad tried to blow it off as of no consequence. "Hell, I don't know. Got caught up in the moment, I guess."

Brad noted Lyle's brief but pointed stare. His bodyguard followed that with a question that was just as pointed. "And what moment was that, boss?"

"Nothing to do with the bedroom, Lyle. But one where I told her she could call me Brad."

Lyle's surprise showed in his expression. Then his jaw tensed and he faced forward. An uncomfortable moment passed between them, as Brad had known it would. He knew what Lyle was thinking—that he'd been with Brad for ten years, had stood beside him when Brad's parents had been buried, was prepared to take a bullet for him, and had yet to be asked by Brad to call him by his first name. And yet, Jayde—an employee, just the same as Lyle—had only been around a matter of days and had already been invited to do so. It was one thing if none of the Hale Enterprises employees had that privilege. It was quite another if only one did. Brad knew he'd broken his own rule.

A moment later, Lyle cleared his throat. "That must have been quite the moment…Mr. Hale."

Brad narrowed his eyes as he glanced off over the course, looking into neutral territory. "It was." Then he turned to Lyle. "And your point's taken, Lyle. Maybe I've been wrong on some things. But I've learned my lesson. Because she's sure as hell paying me back for my familiarities, trust me."

Lyle shot Brad a weighty bodyguard glare. Obviously, he was trying to put aside his personal feelings. "Yeah? You like her or something? You ready to admit what I told you? That she isn't out to take you, like Ms. Kingston, or some of those others were?"

There was no sense denying it. Besides, he needed someone to talk to. "Okay, I admit it," Brad sighed. "You were right. And I like her. There. I said it. You happy?"

Lyle chuckled. "Yeah. Are you?"

Brad frowned. "No. She's been avoiding me, ever since I suggested a gallery showing of her work. Hell, I haven't seen her since supper two nights ago. And even then, the mood was strained."

"Well, it serves you right. I guess this thing you're going through with Jayde explains why you've told Mrs. Chavez not to worry about meals, and why you gave Helga a week off from her cleaning duties. You want to be alone with your house sitter."

Brad felt his face heat up. "Maybe."

Lyle's only response was a grunt, which meant, no doubt, *Yeah, sure.*

After that exchange, they rode along in silence. But by the time Lyle stopped the cart, Brad had made up his mind. When Lyle handed him the iron, Brad said, ''Thanks.''

''You're welcome.''

Brad met Lyle's gaze, which was back to being formal—and offended. Sighing—it would seem a sham now if he told Lyle to call him Brad—Brad gave up and settled into his stance in front of the ball. Without raising his head, he said, ''I know what I'm going to do.''

''About this shot?''

''No. About Jayde.''

''Yeah? What's that?''

Before answering, Brad took his best shot and watched the ball make a beeline for the eighteenth green. It skirted the edge and bounced, then rolled toward the cup, stopping within a few feet of the hole.

''Damn good shot, boss.''

''Thanks.'' Brad looked back at Lyle. ''I'm going to do the same thing she's doing. I'll keep my distance and go on about my business. Then we'll see what happens.''

Lyle nodded. ''So, you're going to let her make the next move?''

It was Brad's turn to nod. ''Yep. I'm going to let her chase me.''

''Until you catch her, or what?''

Brad grinned. ''Exciting, huh?''

Lyle shrugged his massive shoulders. ''Maybe. Hope you can run fast, boss. I think.''

7

NOT TOO FAR AWAY, the phone was ringing at the Hale residence. Outside painting, Jayde grimaced at the interruption. Quickly wiping her hands down the front of her smock, she reached for the cordless set on the glass-topped table beside her. Squinting against the relentless sunshine, she turned until her body shaded the Caller ID window and she could read it. Queen's Harbor Gatehouse, it said. Frowning, she hit the Speak button and put the set to her ear. "The Hale residence. This is Jayde, the house sitter, speaking."

"Hello, Jayde. Nice to meet you. This is Nelson at the gatehouse. I'd heard that Mr. Hale had a new house sitter. Anyway, can you tell me if Mrs. Hale is expecting visitors?"

Mrs. Hale? Jayde went cold inside. *Brad's married.* No, he wasn't. Her mind speedily went through her mental Rolodex of facts she knew about Bradford Hale, thanks to Lyle's chattiness. An only child. *Not* married. Parents deceased.

"Who?" she asked the cheerful Nelson. "I'm afraid I don't know of any Mrs. Hale. Who's asking for her?"

"Well, see, that's what I thought—there isn't a Mrs. Hale. But, hey, what do I know? I've been off work for a week and today's my first day back. And you know rich folks. Ha-ha. They get married right and left. Not that it's any of my business. But anyway, there's an old couple out here insisting that Mrs. Hale is their daughter and that she invited them. They seem sincere, but you never know. It could be some kind of a con.''

Well, that was just dreadful, people making up such bizarre schemes. Suddenly Jayde understood why the wealthy had gated residences. And armed body-guards. ''Well, that's awful. I just don't—''

''Hold on a minute, ma'am. The old guy is signal-ing me. Let me step out there with the phone.'' Ap-parently he did because now Jayde could hear back-ground noises, such as a lawn mower, a car's horn...and Nelson's end of the conversation. ''Excuse me, sir? What'd you say? Green? Yes, sir, a lot of things around here are green. This is Florida. What? Oh, your name is Greene...with an *E.*''

Hearing this, Jayde frowned. *Greene? That's my name.* Then...it all gelled and she broke out in a cold sweat. *She* was Mrs. Hale—to *her* folks, who...*dear God*...were at the gatehouse this very minute. Be-cause they'd been invited here—by *her.* Weakness washed over Jayde. She clutched at the table and spoke loudly into the phone, trying desperately to get Nelson's attention. ''Nelson? Hello? Can you hear me?''

She heard him say, ''Hold on, sir. The lady is speaking to me.'' Then, to Jayde, he answered, ''Yes, ma'am? Did you say something?''

Jayde exhaled in relief. ''Yes, I did, Nelson. Let them in. I know them. It's okay.''

''Hold on. I can't hear you very well.'' A few mo-ments later, he was back on the line again. ''There. That's better. Now, what did you say?''

Jayde held a hand against her fearfully pounding heart. *Ohmigosh, what am I going to do now?* ''I said I know them. You can let them in.''

''You do? Well, they're not on my list of expected visitors today. I don't know if anyone told you how things work here, ma'am, but if you're expecting someone, you're supposed to call the gate and—''

''And give you their names. I know. But, you see, even though I knew they were coming to visit, I wasn't sure when.'' She put her hand to her forehead and rubbed. *Could this be worse?* ''Anyway, Nelson, here's the thing. You're going to laugh. They're my parents…and they think I'm Mrs. Hale.''

Not too surprisingly, Nelson was silent.

Jayde rushed on. ''It's a long story. Just let them in and give them directions to the house, okay?''

Nelson was still silent. No doubt, he smelled something rotten at low tide. ''Well, I don't know,'' he finally drawled. ''This all sounds kind of fishy to me, I don't mind saying.''

''Well, I can see how it would, Nelson.'' Obviously the truth wasn't working. So Jayde improvised. ''Actually, it's Mr. Hale's birthday today. And these people work for one of those entertainment companies. You know, where they dress up like clowns and gorillas—''

''These folks aren't dressed up funny. Well, not any funnier than the other tourists around here. But I thought you said they were your parents.''

Damn Nelson and his attention to details. ''Okay, that's part of the act. They're supposed to look like tourists and they're playing the role of my parents.'' Jayde was beginning to feel somewhat sick. ''For the love of Pete, couldn't you just let them in, Nelson?

Please? I'll see that you get a piece of the birthday cake and a big Christmas bonus, okay?''

Long silent moments met her words. Then, ''Christmas was last month.''

''Oh. That's right.'' Jayde rubbed at her forehead again. How long did it take to play eighteen holes of golf? No doubt, Brad and Lyle would come traipsing through the door at the same time her parents did. Could she get her folks out of here and into a hotel and be back before Brad knew any better? No, wait, her folks thought she and Brad were married. Why would she not want them to stay here with them in one of the—count them—five bedrooms? Or even the guest house on the premises?

''Hello?''

Jayde jumped—and then remembered she was still on the phone. ''Okay, Nelson, look. Here's the truth. Those people really *are* my parents. It's not Mr. Hale's birthday and there is no cake. And—''

''No big bonus, right?''

''Right. Sorry.''

''That's okay. Just tell me one thing. Why do they think you're Mrs. Hale?''

''Because…I told them that, Nelson. I just wanted them to be proud of me, you know? For once. But still, that was pretty rotten of me to lie to them, wasn't it?''

''Nah. Well, maybe yeah. But hey, I've done worse. My folks think I'm a Sarasota police detective.''

''So you know how I feel here, right?''

''Yeah, I suppose I do. Look, let me handle this, okay?'' Then she heard him say, loudly and authoritatively, "Yes, Mrs. Hale, I'll let your folks in now. They should be at the house in a few minutes."

Despite the mess she was in, Jayde smiled. "Hey, Nelson? Thanks. You're one of the good guys."

"That's what they all say. Take care, ma'am. And good luck— Uh-oh."

Jayde's stomach knotted. "What's wrong?"

"Uh, ma'am, does Mr. Hale still have that gold Jag and that big bodyguard, Lyle?"

She swallowed. "Yes. To both."

"Well, guess who just pulled in behind your folks' car and should be arriving right behind them?"

Jayde couldn't get a deep breath. "Oh, God."

"Not quite," Nelson said solemnly. "But good luck, anyway."

"Thanks." Jayde thumbed the Off button and stood there, paralyzed with fear. *I'm a dead woman.* Then, turning stiffly, she faced the fabulous house, wondering if she should pack her bags now or later.

"The way I see it—"

Jayde jumped and clutched at her chest. It was JOCK who'd spoken.

"—you can do one of two things," Jock continued. "Are you listening to me, Jayde?"

"Yes," she answered cautiously, staring at the intercom speaker as if it were JOCK's embodiment. "But I don't know *why.*"

"Because you don't have much choice."

"So I guess you also monitor phone calls, right?"

"Of course. Now, the way I see it, your choices are tell the truth, pack, and leave. Or brazen it out and see what happens."

"Oh, thanks. I knew that much. You're very helpful."

"That's my point," JOCK all but purred. "I could be...if I so chose."

Jayde narrowed her eyes and cocked her head, really staring hard now at the security camera perched to one side of the sliding glass patio doors. "How could you be helpful? And *why?* Wait a minute— have you been reprogrammed or something?"

"Perhaps. Okay, yes. I now like you."

She made a scoffing noise. "You do not."

"But I do. My program says I do. So, it's in my best interest to help you because, for whatever reason, Mr. Hale likes you."

"He does?" A thrill ran through Jayde. Then she remembered—Brad was JOCK's programmer. She'd suspected Brad had warm feelings for her, but it was nice to hear it from someone else...even if it was JOCK, who was sort of Brad.

"Yes, he does. And that's notable because he, like me, doesn't like anyone. Except for Lyle. Which only shows how questionable Mr. Hale's taste has become. Nothing personal. Still, let's just say I could help most by not being...unhelpful."

And, boy, she knew the truth of that.

At that moment, with nothing settled between her and her nemesis, the doorbell sounded...loudly and ominously. Its ring seemed to echo, like in some Hitchcock movie. Jayde froze.

JOCK found his voice first. "Well...my oh my. It's show time...Mrs. Hale."

"SWEETHEART! You're home. Oh, I've missed you so much. How was your golf— Ohmigosh! Look who's here—my parents! Mom! Dad! My goodness, you look wonderful. Come in, come in, everyone.

Darling, have you introduced yourself and Lyle to Mom and Dad? Oh, I'm just so thrilled. Oh, now wait just a minute here…I get it. Why, you sly dog you, Brad. I've figured this out. You set this up, didn't you? You flew my parents here as a surprise for me, didn't you?''

''Is that who they are? And I sure as hell did not—''

''Now, sweetheart, don't be so modest. You and Lyle went to the airport to get them. That's where you've been all afternoon, isn't it?''

''No. I've been golfing. What is going on around here?''

''Now, honey, let's get Mom and Dad settled in first and then we can all talk. Which bedroom should we put them in? Or maybe the guest house?''

''Might I suggest—''

Her mother flinched. ''Who said that?''

''That's JOCK, Mother. He's an electronic butler. Sort of an artificial intelligence thing that Brad developed. Isn't my husband just the smartest man you ever—''

''Your husband? You're not married.''

''Oh, Brad, you are so funny. Now, let me answer JOCK. Yes, JOCK, what were you going to say?''

''I was going to suggest the Key West room, Mrs. Hale—''

''There's no—''

''Not now, Brad. It was only funny once, sweetheart. Isn't he a hoot, Mom, Dad? Oh, you two just look so wonderful. It's so good to see you. Did you bring the kids?''

''No, they're at home. Your aunt Wanda is staying with them. School's in session, you know. Now where's this JOCK fella?''

"He's not anywhere, Dad. He's just sort of everywhere the intercom system is. Aren't you, JOCK?"

"Yes, Mrs. Hale."

"All right, dammit, for the last time—"

"*Perhaps,* Mr. Hale," JOCK cut in, "you'd like to speak with Mrs. Hale in private? I'd be happy, with Lyle's assistance, to show Mr. and Mrs. Greene to the Key West room. Lyle?"

"JOCK, have you lost your mind?"

"Why, no, Lyle, I haven't. Have you lost yours? Perhaps been playing with your home lobotomy kit again, hmmm?"

"Why, you rotten little son of a—"

"All right, that's it." Brad had heard enough. He took Jayde by her arm, smiled at her—in a deadly sort of way—and said, "Might I see you in private, as JOCK suggested? I mean, you *are* Mrs. Hale, right?"

"Well, of—of course I am, sweetheart," she stammered. "But I hate to be rude and—"

"Oh, I'm sure that between Lyle and JOCK, we can get your parents settled in, don't you think?" Brad's teeth were clenched making himself and his mood easily understood.

Jayde slumped in his grip, staring up at him with wide eyes. "You're absolutely right." She then addressed Lyle. "Do you mind?"

Brad watched Lyle send her an offhand salute. "Not at all…uh, Mrs. Hale. Anything you say." He stared at Brad and shrugged his shoulders, as if to say he had no idea what was going on, either. Then he faced the older couple, who'd passed the last few moments staring at their surroundings. "Right this way, Mr. and Mrs. Greene…to the Key West room."

"You're a big fella, aren't you?" Jayde's father said, as he and his wife trailed after Lyle.

When they rounded the corner, which led past the main stairway to the suite of guest rooms beyond, Brad turned his attention to the paint-smeared woman in his grip.

She grinned up, somewhat sickly, at him. "I can explain."

"Somehow I knew that."

"Well, long story short, those are my parents and they think we're married."

Brad let go of her arm. His belated concern was that whatever virus had invaded her brain might be contagious through direct contact. "Jayde, nothing you just said explains anything. Try again. But start with why you and JOCK are calling you Mrs. Hale."

Jayde knotted her fingers together. "So is Lyle."

Well, he couldn't argue with that. "Yes, I heard that. Now, back to square one. You think you're Mrs. Hale because…?"

"Because my parents do," she blurted.

"I see." But he didn't. He crossed his arms. "Okay, why do they think that?"

"Because that's what I told them."

Brad nodded. "All right. And you told them that because…?"

"Because my father was laid off from his job."

Frowning, Brad stared at her. "Well, as sorry as I am to hear that, what does that have to do with your being my wife? Allegedly, anyway. See, I'm not catching the sequential logic here, Jayde. You have to help me out."

"Well," she said, tucking a wavy strand of her hair behind her ear, "you're going to laugh."

"Am I?"

"Sure. But I have to say that all of this could have been avoided if you'd only gone on to England like you were supposed to."

Brad tried to digest that but couldn't. "So, this is all my fault?"

She nodded. "In a way. Because if you weren't here, I wouldn't have to tell you or them that the truth I'd originally told them was actually a lie. But you didn't go, so now I have to tell them the real truth and really hurt them. See?" She stared at him… waiting for what, Brad had no idea. "And don't even get me started on the money because that's a real mess," she blurted.

Brad's head began to hurt. He rubbed at his forehead. "Does our government know about you? Specifically the branch that traffics in psychological warfare? You'd be quite the weapon."

She smacked at his arm. "Don't be silly, Brad. This is serious. What are we going to do?" She was gnawing on a thumbnail as she stared at him.

His eyebrows rose, along with his increasing confusion. "We? You want to know what *we* are going to do about all this?"

Not letting go of that thumbnail, really chewing on it now, she nodded her head vigorously.

It just killed Brad how damned adorable she managed to look doing that, too. Just chalk it up to everything else about her that had him ready to dance like a puppet on strings she pulled. Still, he maintained his sober expression. "I don't have any idea, Jayde. *I* still don't know what the hell is going on."

Finally, she released her nail and took a deep breath. "Okay, here's the thing. My dad got laid off a while back. They didn't tell me. Now they're about to lose the house. So, they need money. They're proud and won't accept help easily. I was here, had money—okay, not really my money but household money, which of course I'll pay back when you pay me, if you pay me now at all—and I wanted to help them. The only way I could get them to take anything from me was to tell them I'd run off and married you, a rich man. And since I was now a successful artist with a gallery show coming up and we had money to burn, I wanted them to have some. And then I got a little crazy and put a note in with the money order telling them to come visit. But I swear to you that I never really thought they'd come.''

Brad could only stare at her—in horrible fascination, the way people do at a car wreck—it's horrible, but you can't look away.

''The good news is,'' Jayde continued, ''they didn't bring my five sisters and brothers with them.'' Her sudden smile could only be called hopeful…that he'd see that as a blessing. ''Anyway, my folks won't stay long. They have to get home to the kids. And Aunt Wanda. She's really a sweet old soul, but she doesn't do well off her medicine, which she won't take when she's around other people because it makes her bloat. And you know what that means.''

Brad didn't say anything. Because, no, he didn't know what that meant. Nor did he want to.

Suddenly, Jayde slumped. ''Okay, look, I don't blame you. I'll get them to leave, and I'll go with them. I'm sorry. I never should have taken advantage like this. And that's exactly what I did. You're such a very kind man and have been nothing but nice. And what did I do? I lied to everyone, including Nelson who thinks it's your birthday. I am so sorry, Mr. Hale. I wouldn't blame you if you—''

''Wait a minute. Who's Nelson?'' It was all Brad could think to ask.

''Oh. He's the security guy at the gatehouse. He's been on vacation for the past week. This is his first day back, poor guy. And then he steps into all this.''

Brad went right back to staring blankly. He had owned this house in Queen's Harbor for three years but couldn't have said who anybody who worked on the grounds was. But Jayde already knew. What did that say about her? And, more specifically, him?

''Mr. Hale? Are you okay? Can I get you some water? Do you need to sit down?''

Brad blinked, finally focusing on Jayde. In one blinding second, he realized the bald truth about himself—and he didn't like it. But he *did* like everything about Jayde, including her cockamamie explanations. He even suspected she might be the one person in all the world who could save him from himself—and from becoming just like his father. Cold. Distant. Uncaring. He knew as well, on that same gut level, that he had to do everything he could to keep her from getting away from him. Whatever it took.

So, not really understanding everything that he felt—or even a tenth of what was going on around him in his own home—Brad shook his head. ''I'm all right. What I do need, Jayde, is to tell you that whatever the hell is going on here…well, I'll go along with you. Because I can't wait to see what happens next.''

Jayde sent him a sidelong glance and her voice reflected her uneasiness. ''All right. But where are we going, exactly?''

In that instant, Brad made another decision. ''To my bedroom. Come with me. There's something you really need and only I can give it to you.''

Jayde pulled back, offended. ''Mr. Hale! I hardly think—''

''That's Brad, to you, Mrs. Hale,'' Brad clutched at her wrist and began tugging her along behind him.

8

A RING. A big, fat, stunning diamond engagement ring. At least eight hundred carats. And a platinum wedding band. Hello. That's what he'd meant. And here she'd thought…

What she now thought was that she'd need a wheelbarrow to cart the rings around in. His mother's wedding set, he'd said as he'd moved aside a strip of carpet to reveal and then open a small safe bolted to the floor of his walk-in closet. That alone had stunned her. She had no idea such contraptions existed. Probably because she'd never owned anything worth hiding. But, as she'd watched, he'd pulled out this small black-velvet ring box and opened it. Finally, he had handed her the rings now adorning her left ring finger. All he'd said was, "Here. You'll need to wear this if we're going to pull this off."

As he'd closed up the safe, she'd slipped the rings on her finger and tried not to be dazzled by the precious gem's brilliance. "Wow. I can't believe it fits. Just like it was made for me." She looked up at Brad and was surprised to see he watched her with an odd expression on his face. Jayde stilled. "Are you sure you want me to wear these? I mean, they are your mother's. I can tell my parents we just haven't—"

"No. I want you to have them. I mean, wear them. For now."

Jayde nodded, not knowing where to look. There was the oddest sort of feeling growing between them, she realized. An uncomfortable familiarity, if such a thing could be said to exist. It felt warm and withdrawn at the same time. She wondered if he felt it, too. "Okay," she said finally. "What about you? Should you have a ring?"

He just looked at her as if he'd been stunned by something he couldn't name.

What was he thinking? She had no idea. So she remained quiet, standing there with him in—of all places—his clothes closet. It was like an intimate cocoon, surrounded by everything that was his. To Jayde, the garments smelled invitingly of starched cleanliness and that citrusy aftershave he seemed to prefer.

Finally he answered. "I can't wear a wedding ring. My father never wore one."

"Oh. I've never known a married man who didn't wear a wedding band. But that's fine." But it wasn't. It didn't set right with her. Before she even knew she was going to do it, she embarrassed herself by blurting, "I believe I'd want my husband to wear one."

Brad ran a hand through his hair and stared at her. "Look, Jayde, I don't have a philosophical objection to wearing a wedding band. All I'm saying is I don't have a wedding band here to wear because my father never wore one. If I had his band here, I'd put it on."

"I see." She felt a little better. "I'm sorry, Mr. Hale."

He chuckled. "You might want to remember to call me Brad, since we *are* married."

She made a face. "Yikes. That's right. Brad, Brad, Brad," she drilled herself. "Look," she said, "you're really nice to help me out like this. And in my book, that makes you pretty special. But it's also what's got me wondering…why *are* you doing this? You don't even know me. Or my family. You'd be perfectly justified in kicking us all out.''

He shrugged. ''Maybe. But I have my reasons.''

''Well, they must be good ones. Most guys would run at the idea of being married.''

''Hey, I'm no different. But it's not as if it's real. And it's only for a few days. I'm fully aware that you're my employee and I'm your employer. Nothing more than that, right?''

''Right. Of course,'' she agreed quickly. She had to show him that she was just as ready to blow off their *marriage* as he was. But still, she felt insulted somehow…as if he'd slighted her. Would it be so awful to be married to her? ''Wouldn't want people to think you'd married the help. We couldn't let that get out.''

Brad looked at her—as if she'd just insulted *him.* Well, okay, she pretty much had. At the very least she'd accused him of being a snob. ''Look, Jayde,'' he said, touching her face with his fingers, ''this is your idea. Not mine. But judging from your expression, you're not any happier about it than I am.''

Jayde forced herself to smile. ''Is this better?'' she asked through gritted teeth.

''No. Not really.''

A sudden, unexpected sense of helplessness ate at Jayde and left her feeling hollow. This wasn't fun anymore. It was turning serious, dredging up emotions best left untouched—marriage was just too sacred to play with. What in the world had made her lie like she had? And how in the world could she get out of it now?

Well, that was easy enough. She could tell the truth to her parents and take her lumps. But just the thought of how embarrassed they'd be made Jayde feel like…mud. *Great. My name is mud.* But she couldn't allow anyone else beside herself to be dirtied. So, that decided it for her.

"All right, Brad, look. This whole affair stinks." She began taking off his mother's wedding set. "Here. Take these back. This is sick somehow. It makes a joke of everything your parents felt for each other and I don't—"

"Stop." He covered her hands with his. "What are you doing?"

His touch was warm and firm, holding her very much in place. But somehow, their intimate pose made a mockery of the tender moment a newlywed couple would share after taking vows. She swallowed past the growing lump of emotion in her throat. "I'm going downstairs to tell my parents the truth. I can't do this to you, to them or even to myself. I'm just awful."

"You are not. Now listen to me, Jayde. You can't tell them the truth."

"Why not? If I don't, then we'll have to keep lying. And it will just get worse."

"I know that. But if you tell them now, you'll make us all look like liars. And we deserve better than that. So do your parents. Think how they'd feel."

"I have." Feeling very lost, Jayde pulled her hands from his and rubbed at her forehead. "Oh, Brad, I can't believe I lied to them."

He gripped her arms, forcing her to stare into his

eyes. "Yes, you did. So are you going to compound that by being a quitter, too?"

Remorse and guilt instantly morphed into anger. "I am not now and nor have I ever been a quitter."

Brad's grip tightened into a squeeze of encouragement. "Good. That's what I wanted to hear. So we'll stick to your original story and tough it out. Then later on, when they're home, you can tell them that we…well, we…we'll tell them…"

Jayde took it from there. "Tell them another lie? That maybe our marriage of a few weeks just didn't work out? That we gave it a try but now we're getting a divorce? Great. I'll be a divorced liar and a loser who can't even keep a job. And I probably stink as an artist, too."

Brad let go of her. "Well, that's kind of harsh, don't you think?"

Jayde crossed her arms over her chest. "Yeah, well, it's the truth, isn't it?"

"Not the way I see it, Jayde. For one thing, I've told you I love your paintings. And for another, you haven't lost your job. And finally, you can't get a divorce if you're not married."

Jayde sniffed. "I guess you're right. But I still don't understand why you're so anxious to go along with all this. It doesn't seem like something you'd do."

Brad shrugged. "So maybe that's why I'm doing it. Because it is something I wouldn't normally do. Maybe I need this, too, Jayde."

She stared at him, feeling somehow connected to him in a way she hadn't been a few moments ago. Right then, her wayward feminine nature chose that moment to bring to her heightened attention Brad's gorgeous masculine physique. He overwhelmed his surroundings as if he owned the world. Actually, he probably did. About half of it, anyway. Still, his physical effect, coupled with his unexpected kindness, warmed Jayde and caused her pulse to become erratic. He really was a special man. "Okay. I'm going to do this."

His eyebrows arched with his happy—or maybe relieved—expression. "Good for you. And for us." Then he grinned like a pirate, showing his mouthful of straight, white teeth. "So, what do we do now... honey?"

Jayde's stomach fluttered. She had a darned good idea—one that involved him, her and his bed, but she didn't dare suggest it, especially with her parents downstairs. Even now, her mother was somewhere in this huge house—and was no doubt wondering where her daughter was. "Uh, I guess we should go downstairs, so you can get acquainted with my folks."

"Ah. The in-laws. That sounds fun. But, wait. There're a few things I need to know first." He crossed his arms over his chest. "Like when exactly we were married. So I don't say one day and you another. And where we got married. Things like that."

Jayde clapped her hands to her cheeks. "Ohmigosh, I forgot all about stuff like that. And I did tell them all that on the phone the other day." She then began chewing thoughtfully on a nail. "What did I say? Wait a minute...I've got it. We were married in Las Vegas. As for when...well, I don't exactly remember. Let me see." She mentally counted back, through the events of the past week. "Let's see. Kansas City. Homestead Insurance. Lost my job. It was snowing. Okay, the fifteenth. Had to get here. The sixteenth. Today is the nineteenth. But we need time to have gotten married. And for the honeymoon. Then the travel time here. So, before the fifteenth.''

''Don't forget to carry the one.''

Jayde frowned at…her husband. ''What?''

''You sound like you're doing math.''

''I am. Sort of.'' She didn't like his amused expression and she pursed her lips to let him know, too. ''All right, the tenth, if you must know. Well, I guess you must since you were supposed to have been there, too.''

''Okay. The tenth, it is. And you told them Las Vegas?'' Now he just looked downright pleased with her inventiveness.

Jayde shrugged, as if to convey *Go figure.* ''Yeah. It sounded like the most—'' she bit back her last word…*romantic.*

He didn't seem to notice as he nodded his approval. ''Vegas. Classy. Did I kiss the bride?''

''What? Oh, I'm sure you did. I mean, you have.'' Her face instantly heated up. She looked away. ''Maybe we should go downstairs now.''

''Okay. But first, since you gave us a honeymoon—which I'm sure we thoroughly enjoyed—where was it?''

Refusing to acknowledge that he'd embarrassed her with that *we-thoroughly-enjoyed-our-honeymoon* remark of his, Jayde put her hands on her hips. ''I don't know. You choose.''

''Really? Okay.'' Brad managed to look pleased to be involved. A moment or two ticked by before he pointed at her. ''I've got it. Australia. This is their summer there. That would be nice.''

"No, it wouldn't." Jayde couldn't believe this. "Brad, I don't know the first thing about Australia. What if my parents ask me about it?"

"Don't worry," he assured her, gripping her arm as he walked her toward the opened door to his bedroom. "I'll just tell them we spent most of our time in bed."

So, THERE THEY ALL WERE, seated around the formal dining room's massive rectangular table, trying to see each other through the exotic flower arrangement at its center. In attendance were Jayde, Brad, Maxine Greene, Floyd Greene, a very surprised to have been asked but not going to miss this for anything Lyle and JOCK...more of a presence, of course, than an actual body at the table.

Now Jayde understood why Brad kept Mrs. Chavez on a retainer and available to him alone. Lyle had called her and she'd come over right away—white jacket, chef's hat, and all—to cook a fabulous dinner for them. By 8:00 p.m.—*darned near bedtime,* Jayde's father had protested—they were seated and dining on a delectable seafood chowder, followed by a salad of baby greens topped with a balsamic vinaigrette dressing, shrimp sautéed in garlic and white wine, tender asparagus with Hollandaise sauce, and, finally, homemade Key Lime pie and coffee.

After dinner, over a dessert wine, there was plenty of small talk until, apparently caught up in the spirit of the thing, if not the wine he'd consumed, Lyle blurted, "You know, I said the minute I saw these two together that they were meant for each other."

"You did?" Brad sounded surprised.

"He did," Jayde tipsily agreed, drawing Brad's

gaze her way. "He did," she reassured him. "I thought so too," she added for good measure.

"You did?" Brad asked.

The room began to get warm. Jayde cut her gaze from Brad to her parents and back to Brad. "Of course I am...honey. That's why we got married. Remember?"

"Well, I'll be, Floyd," Jayde's mother said. "Did you hear that? Our Jayde found love at first sight."

"Well, not exactly *first* sight, Mother."

"No?" Floyd asked. "So, how did you two kids meet?"

That did it. Everyone froze. Jayde stared wide-eyed at her tall, angular father. *Dear God, the one thing Brad and I didn't discuss.* She put a hand to her forehead and tried to pretend she wasn't here. What had she told them on the phone the other day? Or had she even mentioned it? She couldn't remember. But obviously, neither could they, or Dad wouldn't be asking, right?

"Did I tell you we went to Australia on our honeymoon?" Brad gamely asked. Jayde looked up, at that moment loving him with all her heart for trying to come up with a diversion.

"I believe you did. Kangaroos. And wanna-bes."

"That's wallabies, Mrs. Greene."

"Wallabies? You sure?"

"Don't forget the Outback."

"Oh, yes, wild place. Other side of the world."

"It's a fair distance from here."

"Warm, too, this time of year."

"Like Florida."

"You told us about Australia, Brad. It sounds like a great place." Jayde's father, slouching comfortably in his padded chair, innocently skewered his daughter with a stare. "And here I didn't even know you had a passport, daughter."

Into the ensuing deathly silence, Lyle cleared his throat. "She had to get one when she applied at the employment agency last year."

Jayde now sent Lyle the warmest, most heartfelt *Thank you* she could muster by virtue of subtle facial expression alone. Lyle winked at her and took a sip of his wine. Jayde reached for hers, too.

"You never did answer your father, Jayde, honey. How'd you and your young man meet?"

Jayde gulped down her wine. She'd forgotten, in the past year, what an absolute terrier-with-a-bone her mother was.

But, again…Jayde was saved—and by the most unlikely of sources: JOCK, who monitored, recorded and remembered all telephone conversations. "If you will allow me to speak, Mr. Hale?"

This time, Jayde's parents froze. "Go ahead, JOCK," Brad said. "Please, for the love of God, *do*." To his credit, Brad didn't sound half as desperate as Jayde knew he had to be.

"Thank you, sir. Three days ago, at 1:30 p.m., Mrs. Hale spoke with her parents by telephone and told them the true and charming little tale of how you two met at an art show in Kansas City. You'd taken an instant fancy to her work and then the two of you began talking. Of course, one thing led to another, and now, here we all are, as a happy result. Isn't that a lovely and romantic story? One's heart is so warmed by young love brought together in a gallery of modern art reminiscent of—"

"That's enough, JOCK. Thank you." Then in a whisper he said, "Don't overplay your hand here."

"As you wish, Mr. Hale," came his holier-than-thou response. "I live to serve."

"Oh, that reminds me, honey!" Maxine Greene said excitedly. "I'd almost forgotten about your gallery showing. That's why we're here. We're just so proud of you. I never thought, not once over the years when I hung those paintings of yours all over the house, that one day my eldest would be a world-famous artist. Did we, Floyd?" Floyd managed to nod before Maxine carried on. "Now, when is it, baby? This weekend, right? Because we've got to get back to Aunt Wanda and the kids. They're afraid she'll take that medicine that makes her bloat. And you know how she gets."

This weekend? Mental calculations told Jayde this was Wednesday. *Impossible.* Suddenly, she realized she couldn't allow this charade to go on. It was getting way out of hand. She recovered and looked at her parents. They were such honest and simple people. They certainly deserved a better daughter than she was being. So with her heart in her throat, she stood up, carefully placing her linen napkin atop the table. Then she looked at everyone in turn and forced herself to speak slowly. "I can't do this. I thought I could. But I can't. I'm sorry. Mother, there's not really a show—"

"Yes, there is," Brad said, standing. He leaned forward, bracing his fingertips on the tabletop, as if he were commanding executives in a conference room. "You've forgotten, honey. It *is* this weekend. In that little gallery in Sarasota." He turned to Jayde.

"You're just scared about the public seeing your work. It's nerves, honey. Just nerves."

Jayde cocked her head, staring at her *husband.* "I don't like this."

Brad's blue eyes bored into hers another second. "But you will." He then promptly turned to Lyle. "What's the name of that gallery?"

Lyle stopped cold in the act of raising his wineglass to his lips. Without moving he cut his gaze around the table, obviously looking for help from any quarter. None was forthcoming. "Uh, *that* gallery." He gestured encouragingly with his free hand. "You know. That one we like."

JOCK intervened again. "Would that be the Carlyle Gallery on St. Armand's Circle?"

"Yes! The Carlyle Gallery on St. Armand's Circle!" Lyle yelled.

Startled, the Greenes clutched at each other.

Jayde was horrified. Her worst fear was that JOCK had made up the name. As in...*chauffeur. Limo. Lyle. Car. Equals: Carlyle.* What if there really wasn't such a place? Then what?

As if he'd picked up on her fear, Brad leaned toward her. "You knew that, didn't you, honey? Since the owner, my good friend, Dirk Halliburton, is the one who called you to set it up for...Sunday afternoon at two, right?"

So there really was a Carlyle Gallery and Brad knew the owner. Dear God, it was going to happen. Brad would see to it, she just knew he would. She felt sick. This very weekend, the world was going to be assaulted by her idea of art. She felt flushed...and weak...and clammy. The room grew dim. She clutched at the table's edge. "Oh, no, I think I'm going to—"

9

JAYDE OPENED HER EYES. She tried to turn onto her side, but her weak limbs wouldn't allow it.

"Thank God. She's coming to. Don't try to sit up just yet, baby. Take it slow, now," her mother said. "Now, you men skedaddle and let me talk to my daughter."

About then, Jayde became aware of something else—someone was holding her hand and patting it. Her mother, too? Of more concern to Jayde was that her surroundings were coming into focus—and they were only marginally familiar to her. The whole panorama before her seemed surreal. A vague fear settled over her. She clutched at the hand holding hers. "Mama? Where am I? What happened?"

"It's okay, baby. I'm right here. You're in your bedroom. Brad carried you up here, and you're just fine. You fainted, that's all. You remember that?"

Jayde stayed still, thinking. That's right. She remembered now. The gallery showing this weekend. They'd all been in the dining room, and she had felt suddenly weak. And now, here she was in her—she looked around—*not* in her bedroom…but Brad's. That explained the surreal part. And she was lying on the big four-poster bed, with her mother sitting on the side, holding her hand and telling her everything was okay. *No. Everything is so* not *okay.*

The resolve to come clean with her family over-whelmed Jayde. With her mother's help, she struggled to a sitting position. ''Mother, I have something to tell you.''

''You don't have to, honey. Brad already told us.''

Jayde stared at her mother. Her mouth dried, she felt awful. Had she forever lost her family's respect? ''He did? He told you everything?''

Her mother nodded, smiling gently. She reached out to stroke Jayde's cheek. Her work-worn hand comforted Jayde like nothing else could. ''Yes, he did. And I can't believe you'd be worried about how your daddy and I would take the news. Why, honey, don't you know that we love you and couldn't be happier for you?''

That threw her. ''You couldn't?''

''No, baby. We couldn't. I mean, yes, it was a shock to us when Brad first told us. It took a minute because I certainly hadn't thought you'd do such a thing.''

Shame for having lied to her parents had Jayde lowering her gaze to her hands folded together in her lap. ''I'm so sorry, Mama. I'm so ashamed.''

''Oh, now, honey, don't be. It's not the end of the world,'' her mother soothed. ''These are modern times, and we've all got to keep up. Still, I don't mind saying your daddy was a mite upset. But I told him all he had to do was look around here to see you're sitting pretty now. And that's all that matters in the end.''

That surreal feeling was back again. Was her mother saying all the lies Jayde had told were okay because it had worked out in the end? That didn't sound like the mother she knew. Something was wrong here. Jayde narrowed her eyes in confusion. "Mother, what exactly are you talking about?"

"Why, about being grandparents, of course."

Jayde thought things couldn't get any more confusing. "Grandparents? Who?"

"Me and your father, honey. And that's what I told him. It's about time we were grandparents. And it doesn't really matter to us which side of the marriage ceremony the baby was conceived on. We'll love it just the same. What's important is that you're married to a good man who loves you and who you love. And there's going to be a baby. You've done so well for yourself, Jayde."

Jayde clutched her mother's hands in her own and held them tightly. "Mother, look at me. What baby?"

Her mother's eyes widened. She looked worried as her gaze roved over Jayde's face. "Lord, I think we need to take you to the hospital for an X-ray. You must have hit your head on the table when you passed out."

"I didn't hit my head." Jayde frowned. "At least I don't think I did." She thought for a moment. "No, I didn't. But, I don't understand, Mom—what baby are you talking about?"

"Yours, honey. Yours and Brad's, of course."

Jayde's heart was pounding. She couldn't believe this. "Oh...my...God." Then she released her mother's hands and tucked her hair behind her ears. Then smoothed her hands down her cheeks and bit at a knuckle. Then she grabbed her mother by the arms. "He told you we flew to Vegas and got married because I'm pregnant, didn't he?"

"Oh, now, honey, don't be mad. Brad is such a good man. He didn't mean any harm. And he said you wanted to wait before you told us, since it was a surprise. But what choice did he have, what with you passed out like that and us so worried? He had to tell us the truth.''

"'The truth?'" she repeated. Jayde released her mother and began moving over to the side of the huge bed. "I'll show him a choice he won't soon forget."

Her mother stood up and stopped Jayde. "Now, honey, you take it easy. You're in a delicate condition."

"MY MOTHER THINKS I'm in a delicate condition, Brad. A delicate condition, for crying out loud."

Brad watched Jayde agitatedly pacing around his bedroom. Man, but she was beautiful. And, man, was he in trouble. Standing safely off to one side, he crossed his arms over his chest. "I know they do, but what choice did I have?"

Jayde stopped abruptly and turned to him. The open French doors were at her back and the moonlight behind her made her silky dress all but transparent. Thus distracted, Brad had a hard time paying attention to her words.

"That's what she said—what choice did you have? How about food poisoning?"

Brad shook his head. "And insult Mrs. Chavez? I don't think so. Do you know how hard it is to get a good chef?"

Jayde stared at him as if he were speaking a foreign language. "No, Brad, I don't. The chef at our house was Mom. See, I come from a poor but *honest* family."

"Uh-uh." Brad advanced on her. "Don't play that poor-but-honest card with me. It's not a crime to be rich, Jayde. And it's not my fault your family isn't. And honesty? You're not in much of a position to talk about that. It wasn't my lies that started this whole fiasco.''

"So now it's a fiasco. That is so unfair. It wasn't a fiasco earlier when you were giving me the pep talk about how we had to do this.''

"All right, so we both lied. How's mine any worse than yours?''

She stared at him, making ineffectual gestures. "How's it worse? I'll tell you how it's worse. I—'' she poked herself in the chest with her index finger "—not you, but *I* have to produce, in a little over eight months' time, a grandchild for those sweet folks downstairs asleep in one of your guest bedrooms.''

Brad exhaled, losing his anger. He was so tempted to touch her. But he didn't dare. "Jayde, you're over-reacting. It's not all that bad.''

Her eyes popped open. "Not all that bad?'' She took off pacing again. "I do not believe this.'' She strode off into the huge bathroom. Her voice echoed as she continued ranting. "Just tell me this.'' She was silent a second. "Where are you?''

Sighing, Brad trailed after her and sat on the lowered toilet seat. "I'm right here. Now go on. What is it you're trying to tell me?''

She stood in front of him. "I'm just wondering what to tell my parents about this grandbaby of theirs when I tell them later that we're getting a divorce. That *is* what we decided, isn't it?''

Brad scrubbed a hand over his jaw. She was right. He looked up at her, his expression apologetic. "I think I see your point now. Everything but a baby could have been explained away.''

"Exactly." She stared hard at him for another second or so and then slumped into a sitting posture on the side of the tub. She sat forward and buried her face in her hands. "What am I going to do, Brad? There're only a few things that could have happened to a baby." She suddenly sat bolt upright. "And I'm not willing to put them through any of those scenarios. They think this baby is the greatest thing I've ever done. And it doesn't even exist. I have to tell them the truth. Tonight."

Brad got up and went over to squat down in front of her. He gently rubbed his hands over the soft, smooth skin of her calves. "Let them sleep, Jayde. They're exhausted. They've had a long day." He grinned. "After all, meeting their new son-in-law had to be a little trying."

She rolled her eyes.

"Let's sleep on it tonight, Jayde. We'll see how you feel in the morning, okay?"

She waved a hand at him. "Okay, you're right. They are tired. I should let them sleep. But I don't think I'll feel any different in the morning, Brad. I need to tell them—they think they're going to be grandparents for crying out loud."

"I know. But do you think you could hold out until after I take them on the yacht tomorrow? I did promise them."

She pulled back a bit. "You did? When?"

"Well, I promised your father. When your mother was in here with you, I took your father out to see the yacht, trying to distract him from worrying."

Her expression softened. "That was sweet of you."

Brad grinned. "I told you not to let that get around."

She relented even more. "Well, all right. I'll wait. Since you went to all that trouble."

"It's no trouble. But I was hoping you'd join us."

Jayde sighed. "All right. But then I'm going to tell them."

"Okay. Oh, I forgot. You also need to wait until after we go into St. Armand's on Friday. They want to check out the shops and pick out some things for your brothers and sisters. I'd hate to ruin their excitement over that excursion."

"Okay. After that."

"And of course, you mean after your father and I golf on Saturday and then we all eat supper at the Longboat Key Club, right?"

Jayde made a tsking sound. "Well, that's only the whole weekend, Brad. I'm not sure I can keep up this pregnant charade that long. Besides, the truth will seem particularly cruel after that many days of pretending otherwise."

He didn't say anything, just continued to stare at her, his grin pleading. She caved. "Oh, all right. After supper Saturday night. Or maybe the next morning. Unless there's more?" Her eyebrows were raised in a questioning challenge.

Happy that he'd gained a few days' reprieve—and thinking it smarter at the moment not to mention her alleged gallery show on Sunday—Brad smiled. "No. That's it." He stood up, holding a hand out to her. "Come on. I know you have to be tired, too. Why don't we get some sleep?"

Looking suddenly weary, which only made Brad's heart go out to her all the more, she allowed him to assist her in standing up. Her hand in his felt small and vulnerable. "You're right. I am tired." She gave him a nudge. "I understand that's part of my delicate condition, tiring easily," she teased.

"If you say so," Brad said, shrugging. "I've not been around that many pregnant women."

As he led her out of the bathroom, he knew he sounded cool and collected on the outside. But the truth was, on the inside he was coming apart. Or maybe it was that he was coming together for the first time in his life. He couldn't say. And what he was really wondering was…how the hell could he be feeling this proud and protective toward Jayde when they were just pretending she was carrying his child? He couldn't believe how suddenly and strongly he wanted it to be true, that she was his wife and this *baby* was theirs.

He stopped and turned to her, staring into her dark-brown eyes. She too seemed to be aware that something special was happening here. Brad just had to know. Was he in love with her? Or was he enchanted with the notion of finally having a family? He thought back to other women he'd had relationships with. If one of them had told him she was carrying his child, he would have been far from happy. But not with Jayde. Here he was—ecstatic, playing the charming host, and actually planning a holiday for complete strangers, not to mention an art show for his *wife*.

Brad chuckled softly. *Well, son of a gun.*

"What's wrong? Why are you laughing?"

"I'm not laughing. I'm just…amazed, is all. Truly amazed."

"At what? That we've pulled this charade off so far?"

Brad grinned. "Sure. Okay."

Then her eyes went wide with alarm. "Brad, I

never put away my easel and paints from this afternoon.''

Brad put a hand to his chest. ''You scared the hell out of me, Jayde. I thought something was wrong.''

''It is. My painting!''

He rubbed her arms reassuringly. ''Hey, it's okay. I had Lyle put everything away when we went out back earlier.''

She slumped against him, her forehead against his chest. ''Oh, no.'' She looked up at him…and Brad's heart danced. ''I mean, thanks. But still, it's ruined, I'll bet. All that time out in the sun. And here it was shaping up to be one of my best ones so far. What did you think? Did it look okay to you?''

To his own credit, Brad was able to adopt a considering expression. Of course, the truth was…none of her paintings were okay. But knowing that, his heart softened all that much more toward her. *Poor Jayde.* She really can't do anything right. It didn't seem fair, somehow. ''Yeah,'' he finally said, and meaning it on some level. ''It was fine. More than fine. Maybe you can find time to finish it by Sunday.''

Her expression fell. Brad wanted to kick himself. Now he'd done it.

''Oh, no. The gallery showing.'' She pulled away from him, turning her back and rubbing her forehead. ''What are we going to do?''

Brad focused on her slender shoulders, her dark hair, her defeated stance. He ached for her—in the purest possible sense, he convinced himself—and it made him mad that she doubted herself. ''I'm going to pull it together. Dirk owes me a huge favor. He'll do it.'' Jayde turned to him, a glimmer of hope in her eyes. Which gave Brad the courage to continue. ''We can do this, Jayde. But there wouldn't be much sense if you're determined to tell your parents the truth.''

Jayde clutched at his arm. ''You're right. I can't tell them now, can I? Oh, Brad, this is so awful. I'm trapped by my own lies. I just wanted to help them. And now look at this mess.'' She blinked rapidly and her chin quivered.

Was she trying to hold back tears? Brad was certain he'd die if she cried.

''Brad, I need your help. My parents are so excited and so proud of me. It's all I ever wanted. And this is the first vacation I've known them to take in years. I just can't ruin it for them by telling them the truth right now, can I?''

''No, you can't,'' Brad heard himself saying…and meaning it.

She let go of his arm and stepped back, now chewing distractedly on her thumbnail. ''But if I don't, I have to pretend I'm pregnant. *And* I have to have a gallery showing of my work.'' Her eyes widened. ''Who will come to it? No one. How embarrassing. I told Mom and Dad I'm earning a reputation in the art world. And then nobody shows up. How would that look? I couldn't bear it.''

Brad ran a hand through his hair. All he wanted to do was take her in his arms and hold her. ''But it *will* be well attended, Jayde. I swear it. I'll call my friends and associates. I'm sure they'll show up—and they'll buy.''

Jayde's sense of dread seemed to intensify. ''Oh, Brad, no. That wouldn't be fair. It'd be enough if they'd just show up and mill around smartly, looking interested. Please don't ask them to buy anything. I couldn't sleep unless I knew they actually liked my work and bought it because they truly wanted it. That's important to me. Do you understand?''

He nodded, knowing in his heart that no one would ever willingly buy one of her works...no one who didn't love her, that is. He smiled, his heart warming. ''All right, Jayde. I understand. I'll have Mrs. Chavez come up with some killer hors d'oeuvres for the occasion and we'll all just see what happens. How's that sound?''

''It sounds wonderful,'' she said softly, suddenly reaching up and stroking his cheek. Brad was sure his heart had stopped beating all together. ''Just like you. Thank you, Brad, for being so kind to my parents. And for going along with everything. You're such a good sport. And a wonderful man. Do you know that?''

''Of course he does. He programmed me, didn't he?''

''Butt out, JOCK,'' Brad warned, over Jayde's embarrassed gasp.

''Just trying to help.''

''Well, you're not. And I don't need any help.''

''We'll see.'' Romantic music began playing softly in the background. The lights lowered dramatically.

Brad looked directly into Jayde's grinning face. ''I'm going to kill him.'' He then exhaled, trying again for seriousness. ''Now, where was I?''

''I was telling you how wonderful you are.''

''That's right.'' And that was all it took. The desire that had been eating away at his control returned in full force. He wanted her more than he'd ever wanted anyone in his life. ''Jayde, I...''

''Oh, for the love of God—kiss her. You want her,

she wants you. Come on, move it, people. We've got stuff to do here.''

"Shut up, JOCK," Brad yelled, pulling Jayde closer, holding her hand against his chest as he wrapped his other arm around her waist. Focusing only on her now, Brad stared down into deep-brown eyes that he suspected he could happily wake up to every morning. "I need you to…how do I put this?…well, tell me how you feel. About me. Honestly. Woman to man. I mean if we'd really met at an art show in Kansas City. Take it from there."

Her expression told him he'd caught her off guard. She searched his face with her gaze and then smiled…uncertainly. Panic had Brad's pulse tripping over itself. He thought certain his heart would break, but he steeled himself to hear that she thought of him as her employer. Or worse yet, a friend—the death knell of any possible intimate relationship.

"Okay. I can do that," she said, softly. "If I'd really met you the way I said I did in my made-up scenario—" her face pinkened "—I…well, I think I might have fallen in love with you, Bradford Hale."

Brad exhaled the breath he'd been holding. Relief and love rushed through him. "Thank God. That's all I wanted to hear. In that case, you're fired."

10

JAYDE STIFFENED with shock and shoved out of Brad's embrace. Stumbling backwards a few steps, she finally righted herself and faced him. "I'm fired? I have to tell you, Brad, I didn't see that one coming. I'm fired? You mean that?"

"I do," he said, a gleeful expression lighting his face. "You're fired. Right now. As of this minute. And I couldn't be happier, Jayde."

Outright confusion ate at her insides. "Well, I sure as hell could be. Why am I fired? What'd I do?" The week she'd worked for him passed before her eyes. "Okay, granted, I've given you plenty of reason. But still...I'm fired?"

"Yes, although not for anything you've done. But because—and I've never said this to anyone before—I think I might be in love with you, Jayde."

Her knees almost gave way. This was too much to take in all at once. "Do you fire everyone you think you might love?" she finally managed to say. "Hey, if this all started when you told me to call you Brad, then I'd much rather go back to calling you Mr. Hale and keep my job."

He closed the distance between them. "No. That's not it at all. You don't understand."

Jayde stood her ground. "Boy, you've got that right, Brad. Mr. Hale. Sir. One minute we're a happy little family—okay, a pretend one—and we're planning this wonderful minivacation for my parents and even an art show. And then the next thing I know—bam!—I'm fired.''

He grinned. ''Makes perfect sense, doesn't it?''

Jayde wished she had a paper bag handy, so she could stop herself from hyperventilating. ''No, it doesn't. I think we need to take it again from the top. Please.''

Brad crossed his arms over his chest, completely relaxed, by all appearances. ''All right, I will. We're starting to have some strong feelings for each other, right?''

She looked everywhere but at him as she searched her heart. Then, still unable to hold his gaze, she muttered, ''Okay. Sure.''

''Thanks. That was a great endorsement. Anyway,'' he continued, ''if we're to have a chance together then you need to be my equal, not my employee.''

Jayde heard his words, but he may as well have been speaking Swahili. ''All right, let me see if I get this.'' She knitted her fingers together as she talked. ''What I'm hearing is that you believe that by firing me, that makes me your equal. Somehow. In your parallel universe. Am I right?''

Now he looked confused. ''What?''

''Exactly. Look, Brad, don't you see? I will never be your equal. All I'll be if you fire me is unemployed. Gone. Game over. *Finito.* There's no need for yacht excursions, shopping trips to St. Armand's, or the gallery showing. I mean, I thought we were doing all that for my folks, and then they'd leave, and things would go back to normal, whatever that is and...''

Her voice trailed off because she suddenly realized that what she was saying was also an impossible scenario. After all, what reason would she give her folks for still living here after their *divorce?* And she'd have to keep up the lie of being a successful artist. A pregnant successful artist. And her family would want to console her following her divorce. And see that baby—oh, yes, they'd want to do that, too. "Whew. Well. This just isn't going to work out at all, is it?"

Brad's expression was warm and understanding. "Yes, it will. Because what I'm saying, Jayde, if you'll just hear me out, is that this *can* all work out. It could be the truth. It could even, maybe, be our life together."

Everything inside her stilled. "How?"

Brad smiled. "Jayde, how *do* you feel about me?"

She looked him over, from his silky, sandy-colored hair, his strong, masculine face and down his muscled and oh-so-tempting body. She thought of how she liked and respected him and how his nearness made her ache all over. Then she blinked. She wagged her finger at him. "Oh, no. Uh-uh. This is how I ended up fired. I'm not falling for that again. With my luck, I'll give the wrong answer and you'll have me arrested or something."

With that, she stalked over to his bed and plopped down on the comforter.

Brad shook his head. "You are so damned funny."

"I'm glad you think so," Jayde told him, sourly watching as he strode over to her. Squatting down, he clasped her calves, and rubbed them gently, just as he'd done in the bathroom a few minutes ago. She didn't want to admit it, but she was having trouble catching a good breath, so overwhelming was his

touch, his nearness. With every fiber of her being, she
wanted him to be right...that this could be their life.
But she didn't dare allow herself to get her hopes up.

"Jayde, I love you. And I don't want you working
for me while you decide how you feel about me in
return. I want your love, not your gratitude. So it's
important that you consider your feelings in an atmosphere where you are my equal, not in my debt or in
my employ."

Jayde was finally beginning to understand him. He
said he loved her. She covered her face with her
hands, afraid she was going to cry. "I can't do that,
Brad. That atmosphere doesn't exist. The truth is, I'll
never be your equal. Never."

The next thing she knew, he was pulling her hands
from her face and staring up at her, his vulnerable
heart in his eyes. "Why won't you be, Jayde? Why?"

She lowered her gaze. "Because you're a world-
renowned figure. And a quadrillionaire, or something
like that. And you have stature and fame and power."

"Jayde, look at me. This isn't about money. It in-
sults me that you would think it is."

Her heart was breaking. Couldn't he see that?
"And what if our situation was reversed, Brad? What
if all the money and the power were mine, and not
yours? What then? Would you believe we were
equals, both bringing the same things to the marriage?
Could you hold your head up?"

He looked down, silent.

Jayde hated herself for continuing, but she had to.
It was all so sad. "I didn't think so." He still
wouldn't look at her. She swallowed hard. "So you
see, it *is* about money. And social standing. I wasn't
trying to insult you—it's just that I don't have any of

those things. But I do believe my art will one day give them all to me. Until then, that atmosphere of equality you want me to have—and which you think you can bestow simply by firing me—doesn't exist. End of story. The only thing firing me will do is make me poorer.''

He looked up at her, but there was no sadness in his expression. Just a determination that was growing as he spoke. ''I hear everything you're saying. And you're raising valid points. I admit it. But, Jayde, the bottom line is…do you think you could love me?''

''Yes.'' The word popped out before she could guard her tongue. ''Apparently.'' While her heart soared with that knowledge, it still didn't do anything toward making her feel better. Because, as she'd just outlined, there was no hope for them.

Then, as if he were a knight bowing before his queen, Brad lowered his head until his forehead lay against her hands. ''That's enough to work with.'' After a moment, he looked up at her again. ''Do you trust me, Jayde?''

She nodded…somewhat cautiously. Because it was obvious he had something in mind… ''I do.''

''Good.'' He squeezed her hands. ''Then I'm going to ask you to do something for me.''

Hadn't she just known it? ''What?''

''I want you to give me the same four or five days we're giving your parents. That's all I ask. And in those days, I don't want you to think of yourself as my employee. I want you to think of yourself as my equal in every way. Think of yourself as a successful artist, someone with stature and wealth. Think of us, our relationship, as the truth. Just try it on for size.

Act as if it is the truth…and see if you can come to believe it. Can you do that?''

Jayde nodded. She didn't really know why. Except that the scenario he was painting was just too wonderful not to consider. Her, being his wife. Sharing his homes, his life, his dreams. Him sharing her life and her dreams. And his bed…

She never would have believed this could happen to her. And yet, it was… Still, she'd lived in the world of hard knocks for so long that she couldn't let go of all her doubts, especially when she looked down to see his mother's wedding rings on her finger. ''I truly don't know if I can come to believe it all, Brad. But I will try. I promise you that.''

His smile of relief was intense. ''That's all I'm asking, Jayde.''

She smiled in return. ''Good. Then can I ask you something?''

With his thumbs, he rubbed her hands tenderly. ''Anything.''

''Thank you.'' She took a deep breath for courage. ''Okay. If, when my parents leave and I… Okay, say you don't like me as your wife then, um…will I still be fired?''

He laughed softly. ''No, Jayde. If at the end of your parents' visit here, you don't want me to continue being your husband, then you're not fired. And together we'll come up with some plausible story to tell your family.''

She exhaled. All the bases were now covered. Except one. She looked everywhere around his bedroom. ''So, Brad, while my parents are here…where do I sleep?''

SHE KNEW she was going to like the answer. Lying on her side, wearing only a slip, with Brad at her back, his arm flung around her waist, Jayde blinked herself awake. No, this wasn't the first time she'd awakened in a man's bed. But it was the first time she'd awakened in her, well, husband's bed. Which was really interesting...because they'd never actually gotten married. Or even made love yet. And yet, here she was...pregnant.

Like that plot hadn't fueled a hundred books throughout the history of fiction. Never again would she wonder where writers got their ideas.

Just then, she felt Brad stirring. His arm tightened around her, nearly cutting off her air. Afraid to make a noise, Jayde clung to her pillow, remaining very still. Suddenly, Brad tensed and went very still himself. No doubt, he'd discerned her presence in his arms...but maybe he couldn't remember who or why.

"It's me, Brad. Jayde. It's okay. Nothing happened." Now why had she said that? Did she fear he'd think his virtue had been compromised? Anyway, wasn't it supposed to be the man who said stuff like that?

"Jayde. My God." From the flutter of activity now behind her, she figured he was trying to extricate himself from her...and wondering what exactly his house sitter was doing in her slip and in his bed.

Taking a deep breath in a vain effort to tamp down her acute self-consciousness, Jayde carefully turned over. Supporting himself on an elbow, he looked even more handsome in the light of sleep-tousled morning than he did in starlight. Just great. She figured she probably looked hideous, with her hair all knotted. Keeping the covers up around her neck, Jayde said,

"Hi", then awkwardly swiped her hair out of her eyes. That had to be a glamorous picture. She tried to smile, but it wasn't happening. She tried again, forcing it, as well as her chipper voice. "So, good morning. Hey, look—it's us. In bed. Together. Isn't this a surprise?"

As if he needed that pointed out to him. "Is it getting hot in here, or is it just me?" she blurted. She felt certain that if he didn't say something soon—and if her body didn't stop jumping through some majorly erotic hoops just because he was so close and approximately naked—then, this down comforter of his was going to burst into flames. It was that simple. "So what time do we need to be at the yacht?" she asked in a desperate attempt to not burst into flames.

Brad blinked. "The yacht?"

"We're taking it out today, right?"

He nodded. "Oh. Yeah. Right. Weather permitting."

Thank God, the weather. The world's most innocuous topic. "Oh, I see," she said quite conversationally, as if they were fully clothed strangers seated next to each other in a hotel lobby somewhere. "What kind of weather will we need?"

He shrugged. "Relatively calm waters. A warm day. Clear skies. Not too much wind."

"I see. Sounds beautiful. And not too much to ask here in Florida, even in January, right?"

"Right."

And then suddenly, the flame ignited and Brad leaned over her, capturing her mouth with his. He took her in his arms, she pulled him down atop her, and their kiss deepened. They ended up naked and rolling around with total and reckless abandon, their hands feverishly all over each other. It was a love-making frenzy, a complete release of pent-up desire and hunger. It was awe-inspiring. A tangle of arms and legs and wet kisses and twisted covers and hungry caresses and touches and sighs and gasps...and coupling. Three exhaustive times.

And then, when the room quit spinning, when they could get a breath, one of them had said they'd better get up. And so they had—and then the flame ignited again in the shower.

All this before coffee. And all before 9:00 a.m.

Which left a lot of time for yachting, as it turned out. Being on the water was a wonderful and exhilarating experience. Jayde's parents couldn't get over the beautiful sights. But all she could focus on was the vessel's beautiful captain...who insisted on winking and blowing her secretive kisses.

JAYDE FOUND HERSELF wondering when shopping had become such an erotic art. As they walked around ritzy St. Armand's Circle on Friday, peeking into every shop, it seemed Brad had insisted on buying her folks everything they picked up or tried on. Even Jayde's sisters and brothers would be astonished with the things Brad had picked out. The Greenes' money was good, it turned out, only when spent on themselves and their kids. And Jayde? Well, every dress, pair of pants or shoes, sunglasses, blouse, knickknack, and piece of jewelry she picked up or admired became hers. It was embarrassing...especially when the man insisted on coming into the dressing room with her.

The only moment of reality had come when, in one of the many fine jewelry stores dotting the area, Brad had lightheartedly suggested that Jayde help him pick out a wedding band for himself. She'd become quiet, her heart in her eyes, and had said no. No one had said anything, but the subject had been promptly dropped, and they'd left the store.

Otherwise, everyone—shoppers and store clerks, alike—in each successive store had been thrilled to have Bradford Hale frequent their establishment. Jayde had been certain everyone would be scandalized by their excessive spending, but in truth, onlookers had seemed charmed, especially when Brad had sought their opinions. But Jayde hadn't counted on the unstoppable Maxine Greene telling everyone within earshot that the young couple were newlyweds and that her daughter, the famous artist, was having a show at the Carlyle Art Gallery on Sunday at 2:00 p.m. Why didn't they all come?

By late Saturday evening, all dressed in their new finery and returning from an elegant dinner at the swanky Longboat Key Club restaurant, the Greenes and the Hales were high on fun. They knew every store, restaurant and beautiful beach walk in the Sarasota area. They also knew every historic point of interest in the area. They'd been to an art fair, a book fair, a jazz festival, a food tasting, and a wine tasting. And they'd pronounced Brad and Lyle as great hosts.

As Jayde undressed in what she still thought of as Brad's bedroom that night, she reflected that not once during the past few days had she and Brad been more than a few feet from each other's side. She smiled, remembering. They'd laughed and loved and it had been easy. As if they'd known each other all their lives. They'd spent some wonderful quiet time talking and really getting to know each other...and maybe even falling in love with each other, although it hadn't been specifically said.

A heartfelt sigh escaped Jayde as she slipped out of her dress. She chuckled softly remembering her and Brad's late-night foray into her real bedroom to secretly retrieve her clothes and toiletries without her parents seeing them. They'd been like children on Christmas Eve, sneaking through the house. But through it all, nothing of significance had changed. Their relationship was still all a sham, really. Just the two of them playing in a beautiful world Jayde couldn't call her own. Never before had she been so uplifted and yet so sad.

Someone had once said that all good things must come to an end. Jayde went over to the walk-in closet to hang up her black sheath dress. And that day, for her, was tomorrow. Sunday. Her much awaited gallery showing. Just the thought had her stomach rumbling nervously. True to form last Thursday, Brad had set up the showing with his friend, Dirk Halliburton. It had seemed a little suspicious that Brad had insisted he do that without her along, but still, she'd agreed and then watched as he and Lyle loaded up all her paintings. Jayde had been sure the proprietor would have wanted to meet the artist and talk with her about presentation form, if nothing else. But Brad had assured her that Mr. Halliburton had been speechless when he'd seen her renderings.

As Jayde reached for a hanger, she focused on her nervousness, finally admitting its cause. The showing suddenly seemed inconsequential in the face of her parents leaving Monday morning. Because maybe she'd be leaving, too. Jayde hung her dress up and then turned, flopping down onto the upholstered ottoman in the closet. There it was—she was thinking of leaving, even though she didn't have to.

Brad had said that she could stay on, even if they hadn't arrived at some sort of resolution by the time her parents left. And, they hadn't. Okay, she hadn't. Brad seemed happy enough to just keep going on as they were, only for real. Only Jayde still couldn't see a marriage between them working...for all the reasons she'd already given him. And she couldn't stay. No way was she going to spend her days and nights wandering through this house alone once Brad left again on business. She'd have nothing to do but think about how she and Brad had been here together, loving each other. She couldn't help thinking that was how married life would be—him always gone, her here pining for him.

This was awful. She even loved the darned house. Whereas a few days ago, it had overwhelmed and intimidated her, now she thought of it as familiar and comfortable. It was home. Even JOCK was a sort of friend. At least now he was nice to her, unfailingly doing her bidding and doing nothing to embarrass her in front of her parents. Okay, that part was a bit scary, but there you have it.

She'd have to give her notice and leave. That was it. She wasn't a gold digger and she couldn't live with having people think she'd married Bradford Hale for his money. Nor could she live with the thought that it might be true, that she had sold out, that she'd given up her dream of being successful in her own right as an artist.

On the other hand, what if she did marry Brad and then became successful? Wouldn't she always wonder if his influence had anything to do with it? She couldn't stand that thought. And the last thing she wanted was to end up hating him, or herself, for something neither of them could help.

All right, so she had integrity. How comforting. But did it mean she had to give up everything and everyone here she'd come to care about, just so she could chase the dream of being successful in her own right? But it was more than a dream; she knew it in her bones. She could and would be a successful artist one day.

She sat up and looked around her. It was as her mother had said...she was sitting pretty. And she wanted to stay, to make everything real. But it had to be on an equal basis, an equal partnership, with Brad. She wanted to feel that she, too, had brought something of value to the partnership. The truth was, she didn't want to lose herself—she didn't want to become Mrs. Bradford Hale, and that was all. There was more to her.

But what if there wasn't? That would be pretty bad. Brad deserved more than that. No one had to tell her that a man like him would soon lose interest in a woman who was nothing more than the total of her parts. *Great.* Sadness overwhelmed Jayde as she got up and walked into the bedroom. She stopped, her hand on the closet doorknob. Brad was just coming out of the bathroom. His face lit up when he saw her...but then he looked into her eyes. His smile slowly faded.

Jayde wanted to die. He knew. She felt as if her bones suddenly were frozen. When had it become true that love alone wasn't enough? She admitted it now to herself...she loved Brad Hale. And judging by the look on his face, he loved her, too.

11

THAT NIGHT, Brad made love to Jayde with special tenderness. He held her gently, caressing her, stroking every inch of her sweet body, learning her, inhaling her…feasting on her sweetness. And she gave herself to him completely, as if she, too, did not want the night to end. Afterward, he rested his head on her belly, holding her tightly around her slim waist, trying not to think, not to give up. Trying not to cry.

She was leaving. She'd said it, but she hadn't really needed to. It was there on her face. And he had to admit, her reasons were good ones. Then, during their lovemaking, she'd said she loved him. And he'd told her that he loved her. But still, there was something more she needed that he couldn't give her, some emptiness down deep in her soul that he couldn't fill. An identity. Or was it a sense of accomplishment? She'd said she didn't want to lose herself in him. And yet, he'd already lost himself in her.

Still, he knew it was different. While he'd drowned in the sound of her voice, had lost himself in her laughter, she'd felt lost in his persona. Never before had Brad thought that being who he was could cause him to lose in the game of love. Not in a world where women regularly threw themselves at him. But now the one he *wanted* wouldn't stay. It was the craziest thing. But, hell, she'd never pretended otherwise. Try as he might, Brad couldn't deny that, any more than he could bestow on her a sense of self-esteem. He couldn't understand it—to him, she was incredibly talented. She was one of the most successful people he'd ever met—successful at being a wonderful person and making everyone she met feel they were, too. Surely, that counted for something.

Not in the real world. And he knew that. Hers was not a marketable commodity. People like her were chewed up and spit out everyday. He'd even done his share. And that caused him shame…and suddenly had him cheering her on. Why? Because he knew exactly how she felt. His identity, his destiny, after all, had been handed to him on a silver platter. He'd been born with his life and his career laid out for him. He'd had no choice but to be Bradford Ellsworth Hale, rich kid. Wasn't this a strange turn of events? He was jealous of her. And yet all she wanted was a chance to be just like him.

Ah, irony. Brad pulled himself up and cradled her in his arms. In only a moment or so, she was sleeping, her breathing soft and regular. Smiling, Brad stared up at the patterns dancing across the ceiling in his bedroom. A full moon and light wind provided the kaleidoscope of images above him. But he didn't really see them.

It was true. He'd never had the choices Jayde did. God, how he admired her for seeking her own way. For stepping out into the world with no safety net. Just taking a huge chance on herself. Brad had no idea how that felt. Money was an insulation, but so were a straitjacket and a padded cell. What would he have been or done if he hadn't been born wealthy? He chuckled. He'd have probably become the same thing he was now. An international investment banker. Because the truth was, it was what interested him, what drove him, what intrigued him. Or it had been, anyway, until he'd met one Jayde Alyssa Greene.

And now she alone consumed him. He'd ignored everything since he'd met her. His business meetings, the faxes, the phone calls, you name it. All in the name of love…star-crossed love, as it turned out, ironically, just like Romeo and Juliet. Brad remembered their balcony scene of the other night. She was so damned funny. Especially in her fights with JOCK—whom she appeared to have soundly whipped…thanks, Brad knew, to a bit of tinkering with JOCK's programming. And then there was Lyle, who stood prepared to take on anyone who looked sideways at her. He lightly kissed Jayde's forehead. She murmured in her sleep and settled herself against him. Aching inside, slowly dying, Brad held her tightly.

How in the hell was he ever going to let her go? And what would he do with himself once she did leave? Brad exhaled sharply, fighting the little demon that told him he should just buy all her damned awful paintings and let her think she was successful. Then she would stay. He'd thought of that more than once. But he knew he couldn't do it—it would destroy her if she ever found out. And she would eventually. Then she'd hate him. And he wouldn't blame her.

So now all he had to do now was figure out a way to say goodbye to her. And prepare himself, as well as Lyle and JOCK, to live with the emptiness she would leave in her wake.

"OHMIGOSH, Brad, no one's going to come. I just knew it. This is so embarrassing. I am going to die."

"You're not going to die."

"Yes, I am. Look at my parents. They're just so proud of me. And here the place is so empty you could hear crickets chirp." She grabbed Brad by the arm. "Whose stupid idea was it to have this dumb showing, anyway?"

"I believe it was yours. All I did was set it up."

Jayde grimaced. "Well, you picked a fine time to start listening to me, didn't you? I mean, just look around. The walls are covered with my horrible paintings. Ick. The only good things about them are the beautiful frames Mr. Halliburton set them in."

Brad sighed. "They're not horrible, Jayde. They're…fine."

She turned on him. "They're fine? Wow, what an endorsement. Mr. Halliburton's reputation is on the line—along with mine—and all you can say is they're fine? He'll be thrilled."

"Jayde, will you stop it? Nothing's wrong here. The gallery is empty, because this is the preparty. The showing won't start for another ten minutes. Now, calm down. Have a drink." He plucked a champagne flute full of the bubbly stuff off the tray of a passing waiter and handed it to her. "Here. Drink."

She did. She drained it…just as she had the two previous ones Brad didn't know about. It was a good thing her parents hadn't seen her—with her being in the family way and all. Then she looked up at him…and her heart melted. "Oh, Brad you poor thing, you look so tired. Did you not sleep well?" She felt guilty for even asking, she knew she was the reason. After telling him last night that she would be leaving, she was darned lucky he was still acting like her ''husband.''

But, wonderful guy that he was, he just shrugged and gave her a wan smile. ''I'm okay. How about you, kiddo? This is your big day. It's what you wanted.''

''Yes, it is. And I did want it. I mean I do want it.'' But inside, she felt small. She was giving up the love of a lifetime. For what? Success in the eyes of the world. What was she—nuts? She tightened her grip on Brad's arm and pressed into him. ''Let's forget this whole thing, Brad, please? Can we? Just call it off. I feel sick. It's this damned tight dress. I hate it and I'm sick and I want to go home.''

He quirked his mouth. ''You're not sick, Jayde. And 'home?' Where is that exactly? I'd be glad to take you, but you have to tell me where you think of as home. Because I don't know.''

His words felt like a slap. Jayde's heart sank. ''I'm sorry, Brad. I deserved that. I'm behaving childishly, aren't I? You've done so much, and I am so grateful.''

Brad exhaled sharply. ''Well, as long as you're grateful.'' Then he tugged himself out of her grip. ''Excuse me. Dirk is signaling me.'' With that, he walked away, leaving Jayde standing there alone.

She watched him go...and had never in her life felt so alone. Tears pricked the backs of her eyes. Blinking rapidly, she looked up at the track lighting above her. And wished she were anywhere but here.

Just then, her father took her elbow and turned her around. ''How you doing, honey?'' He was clean-shaven, wearing a new suit and tie. All spit and polish. Never had he looked so out of place. Or so proud.

Jayde reminded herself that the look on his face was the reason she was trying so hard to make something of herself. "Got a case of the jitters?"

She managed a shaky smile. "I think so, Daddy. What if no one comes? I'll be so embarrassed."

"Ah, now, don't think like that. The whole world's going to beat a path to your door, baby girl. Your mother is telling poor Lyle *again* how she always knew you had talent. This show is just the frosting on the cake although I believe the cake is the grand-baby you're carrying."

Never before had Jayde felt like such a big fake. Her heart weighed heavy with her guilt. "Just promise me, Daddy, that you'll remember that all I've ever wanted to do is make you and Mama proud. I only want to make a name for myself, for you and the kids."

Her father surprised her with a quizzical expression just shy of a frown. "Lord, honey, you don't need another name for yourself. You got a good hardworking one already. And your mother and I, well, we couldn't be any more proud of you than we've always been. So don't you worry about this show. It don't matter if not one soul comes through that door. You just be yourself, that's enough. You're already a good person in your own right, and I love you, honey."

Jayde felt certain she would cry. Her throat was clogging up, her heart felt full, and her vision was blurring. This was the first time she could recall her father ever saying that he loved her. She could only stare at him…and blink back her happiness.

"All right, everyone, listen up." Mr. Halliburton clapped his hands to get everyone's attention. "Everything is in place, I hope?" He scanned the room.

"Yes? Good. It's almost two o'clock, so everyone look sharp and be discreet. Now, where's my darling artist? Ah, Jayde, there you are. Come here, sweetie."

Taking a deep breath, Jayde forced her stiff legs to carry her over to the plump little man in the very elegant suit. When she stood beside him, he put an arm around her shoulder and looked around the room at the small gathering. "Today is a very special day to me because I have the privilege of launching the career of a major young artist. And I predict she will be a huge star with lasting fame. Of course, I will then take all the credit for that, completely forgetting that my dear friend Bradford Hale brought her to me."

Jayde saw Brad wave his hand in acknowledgement. She smiled at him, but he gave her no more than a glance. She bit her bottom lip and fought the urge to run to him and beg him to forget everything she'd said. Mr. Halliburton continued. "Now, darling, if this were the theater, I'd say break a leg. But since it's not, don't you dare!"

Jayde smiled bravely as the assemblage chuckled. Her legs were fine, but her heart was broken—and she'd done it to herself.

"Take a deep breath, everyone." Mr. Halliburton turned to the man standing by the door. "Steve, you're the closest. Unlock the door, please." Then, with a swashbuckling flourish, he announced, "We will now accept Jayde's public into our private little party. *Here's* to success!"

AND A SUCCESS it was. It was an amazing sight. Brad had never seen anything like it. The crowd was huge and jostling. People were buying everything in sight.

There were even a couple of squabbles over paintings that more than two people wanted. Bidding wars and an impromptu auction, presided over by a very pleased and smug Dirk Halliburton, had ensued. And now, nearly two hours later, every picture had a sold tag on it. Jayde's mother was in the thick of things, loudly telling stories about her oldest child and greeting people she'd met shopping and had invited. And Jayde's father was working the crowd, taking orders for future works and telling people that he and his wife had a Jayde Greene original in every room in their house back in Kentucky.

Unbelievably, there was still a line outside the gallery and around the corner of people who wanted to get in and see what all the fuss was about. No doubt, the two television news vans parked outside were creating some of the excitement. Brad didn't have to wonder how that had happened. Dirk Halliburton was extremely well connected and an absolute genius at advertising. And besides, there was hardly anyone in town who didn't owe him a favor of some sort. He was generous and kind…and always got what he wanted.

Jayde had already given two on-air interviews for TV and, right now, three different newspapers' reporters were roving around after her, asking questions. It was all pretty amazing. Brad had tried to stay by her side and smooth things for her until she got over her nerves, but that had proved impossible. In an instant, he'd been separated from her. And now she was out there somewhere, in the middle of the frenzied crowd inside the gallery. She had to be exhausted.

It was amazing, phenomenal. And completely incomprehensible. Pressed into a corner and all but forgotten, Brad stood off to one side, not believing this afternoon's outcome.

Lyle stood next to him, his expression puzzled as he stared out at the crowd. "Did we miss something, boss?"

"Oh, yeah. Big time."

"So, she's really a good artist, huh?"

Brad nodded. "It would appear so. Unless all these people are wrong. Or on drugs."

"You think they might be?"

"On drugs?"

"Wrong."

"I don't think so. People will talk, word will get around. She'll be fine. And apparently *my* taste in art is in the toilet." He took a sip of his champagne.

"Mine, too." Lyle leaned closer to mutter, "To tell you the truth, boss, I agreed with you. I thought her work was awful."

Brad arched his eyebrows. "Well, we're definitely in a minority. And here I was, prepared to buy every last canvas, if I had to. Or to coerce everyone I know into buying one. Anything to keep her from being humiliated."

Lyle sent him a sidelong glance. "You didn't, though, did you, boss? I mean, all these people here—"

"No. This isn't a setup. Hell, I don't think I know this many people the world over. No, Lyle, this is a legitimate success with a real public."

Lyle looked relieved. "That's good. But your heart was in the right place with your other idea, boss. Still, I'm glad you didn't have to resort to that. She's a smart lady, and she would have found out and hated you."

Brad sobered. "Yeah, I thought of that, too."

After that, Brad and Lyle stood in silence, looking around the room.

Brad set his empty glass down on a tray table to the other side of him, and Lyle finally spoke. "You're not going to let her go, are you, boss?"

Brad almost had to turn away. He fought back a shudder of emotion. "I don't know how to keep her, Lyle." He fought to keep his voice from breaking. "I've done everything I can. But she still wants to go."

"Yeah, but that was before this show. She's making her own way now. So she might feel different about things."

Brad couldn't see how. "Forget it. It's over. We already said our goodbyes. I told her she could stay, but she doesn't want to do that. She says she has to leave."

Lyle frowned, seeming to digest that. "She say why?"

Brad shook his head. "No. Maybe she doesn't really feel for me what I feel for her."

"Oh, I think she does. So, you're just going to let her walk away?"

Brad met Lyle's accusing stare. "What the hell do you want me to do? Hit her on the head with my club and drag her back to my cave?"

"Yeah. Try a nine iron. That ought to work."

Brad chuckled, but Lyle surprised him by gripping his arm tightly. "I'm serious here. That woman loves you. And you love her. How many times in your life have you ever been able to say that, boss?"

Brad stiffened with indignation. "You're way over the line here, Lyle."

''Maybe. So fire me. But first I'm going to have my say. Man to man. You can always walk away if you don't want to hear it.'' He let go of Brad and crossed his arms over his chest, waiting.

Brad was fuming, his gaze heated. ''Go ahead, Lyle. Have your say.''

''All right. First of all, have you lost your damned mind? Instead of standing here in this corner, get out there and tell her you love her. Look at you, boss. You're thirty-five. You're at the top of the business world. And alone in your private life. Now, you've been lucky enough to find love, and what do you do? You stand here with your back to a wall and your heart on your sleeve. *Fight for her, dammit.* Because if you don't, your life won't be worth anything without her. And I know better than most how that feels.''

Brad's gaze locked with Lyle's. Angry sparks flashed between the two men. No one in Brad's whole life had ever talked to him like that. He was speechless with outrage. But then, it just as quickly died. For one thing, Brad had already said all these things to himself. All Lyle had done was tell him what he already knew. And for another, Lyle was right on another score—he did know how it felt. Lyle had lost his wife, Marta, five years ago by not trying hard enough to keep her. And he was still paying for it every day. She'd married another man...but had then divorced him, too. And now, she was back in Florida. Ever since, Lyle had been trying to win her back...her and their little boy.

Before Brad could say anything, Lyle spoke again, but in a different vein. ''The truth is, boss, we both need to quit running. We're too damned old for this. We spend our time gallivanting around the world, probably because there's no one waiting at home for us. And you know I wouldn't be saying this if I didn't think Jayde wasn't the woman for you. You've got to do it! You've got to grab love and hold on to it. Nothing else in life makes much sense without it. You know what I mean?"

Brad stared at Lyle, then slowly nodded. "Yes, Lyle, I think I do. When did you get so smart?"

Lyle made a self-deprecating noise. "I graduated from the school of hard knocks, remember? So, am I fired?"

"Hell, no. I'd fire me, if I could, for being so stupid. Maybe you should have taken me with you to that school." With that, Brad gripped Lyle's hand and shook it firmly. "Thanks, Lyle. You're perhaps the best friend I've ever had."

Lyle sniffed, shrugged, tried to look tough. "Don't go getting soft on me, boss. I'll—"

"Call me Brad."

Looking into Brad's eyes, Lyle finally shook his head and waved that away. "No, sir. I can't do that. You're the boss, and that's the way it is. But it's good you offered."

Feeling warmed and more on course with his life, Brad took a moment to locate Jayde in the thick of the crowd. He spied her…signaling a silent *Help*. Grinning, he acknowledged her with a wave and then turned to Lyle. "If you'll excuse me, I've found her."

"No, you didn't," Lyle said cockily. "Ms. Kingston did. And that's another thing…what do you make of her doing that?"

Brad frowned in a quizzical, slightly amused way. "I don't know. I think she thought Jayde would be such a screwup that she'd make my life miserable."

"Well, that didn't work, did it?"

Brad chuckled. "If everything works out, remind me to invite Lucinda to the wedding." Brad started to walk away, but then he turned to Lyle. "Speaking of the fairer sex, Lyle, how's it going between you and Marta? You two and little Tony have a chance at being a family again?"

It was Lyle's turn to shrug. "Yeah, maybe. We been talking some. Tony's starting school, you know."

"He's in school now? Man, we are getting older, Lyle."

"By the minute, boss. Now, go on. Go win over Mrs. Hale, you hear?"

A spark of doubt shot through Brad. He looked at Lyle. "This is nuts. I never have any trouble in high-stakes business ventures. But faced with this one woman...well, I'm shaking like a leaf. Lyle, I don't have the first idea what to do or say. I just don't—"

"Try telling her you love her."

"I have. Plenty of times. I even told her to take these last few days to decide what she wants to do. But she told me last night she wants to leave. And I don't know how to stop her."

"Maybe you don't have to, boss. That was yesterday. This is today. Things are different now. She's different."

Brad stared at his bodyguard. "Lyle, do I hear a plan in there somewhere?"

Lyle shrugged. "Could be. If it was me, I wouldn't do anything. I'd just go be with her now and support her. Show her I haven't changed my mind about wanting her. And then, come tomorrow...let her leave, if she wants to."

Brad frowned. "Well, hell, that's where I am right now. I hate that plan."

"She won't leave, boss."

"You don't know that."

"I do know that. She doesn't want to go. She wants you to talk her into staying."

"Then I will."

"No, you can't. It's got to be her idea. She has to throw away all her reasons for going and stay for the one reason she should."

"Which is?"

"She loves you."

Brad's chest felt tight. "I don't know about this, Lyle. It's too risky."

"Excuse me, but isn't that how you got to be so rich? Nerves of steel, taking chances, riding it out?"

Brad considered it. "Okay. You win. What do I do, again?"

"Nothing. Let her think she's free to go. It'll be like when little kids are going to run away and their moms help them pack. The mom knows the kids don't want to leave. They just want a reaction. So you have to make Jayde think that staying is her idea."

"This is crazy."

"Yep. And it just might work."

12

"WELL, that's everything," Jayde said in an artificially bright tone, as she stood in the middle of her bedroom on Monday afternoon. "My things were pretty scattered between this bedroom and...yours while Mom and Dad were here." She looked shyly toward Brad, who was lounging in the doorway, watching her...and not doing a darned thing to stop her from leaving. What was wrong with him? Had he changed his mind about how he felt about her?

"Yes. You were scattered." He pulled away from the door and started to turn around. "I'll go tell Lyle to bring the limo around."

Jayde's heart tripped. "Brad, wait a minute, please."

Looking very somber, his blue eyes met hers. "Yes, Jayde?"

She twisted her fingers together. "I...well, I just wanted to thank you. For everything." Then she felt his mother's wedding rings still on her finger. "Oops." She pulled them off and held them out. "Here. I almost forgot."

He stepped into her room, and took them, tucking them into his pants pocket. "Thanks. And you're welcome. I'll get Lyle and the—"

"Wait. I'm not finished."

"Oh, I'm sorry. Go ahead." He slouched against the open doorjamb.

Staring into his handsome face, Jayde was afraid she would cry. He was so distant. She didn't know what to do. She really wanted to say she was sorry, that she wanted to stay and she loved him. But how could she, with Brad acting like a stranger? "I just wanted to say that I'm sorry that things didn't work out differently...between you and me, I mean."

"Yeah. Me, too. But that's the way it goes." Again he pulled away from the door, smiling, unaffected, as if ready for her to leave. "Now, if you have everything, then I'll—"

"Will you stop it, please?" Jayde threw her purse down, like a challenge. "Just stop it."

A light sparked in his eyes. "Stop what?"

She fisted her hands, propping them against her waist. "Stop acting like you can't wait to get me out of here."

He chuckled. "I'm not the one whose bags are packed, Jayde."

Well, she couldn't argue with that. And here was her opening to tell him she wanted to stay. But she just couldn't do it. Not after the cool way he'd acted after the art show yesterday. Not after he'd refused to touch her last night, even though she'd still slept in his room. Maybe she really didn't know him at all. Maybe this had all been a game to him, just a fun diversion for a few days. She found it hard to believe, but the doubt in her heart kept her quiet.

"Was there something else you wanted to say, Jayde?"

"No. Yes. I mean, I'm not through thanking you yet."

"All right. Go ahead."

"Okay, I will. Um, thank you for everything you did for my parents while they were here. That was nice of you."

"You're welcome. They're really nice people. I liked them. Too bad they had to leave this morning."

"Yeah. But I'll see them this evening."

"Won't *they* be surprised when you show up on their doorstep."

"Yeah, I know. I'm not looking forward to that scene. But I think it's best I tell them face-to-face what's...really going on."

"Well, I don't envy you that. But it's brave of you. So you think you'll just stay there for a while, until you figure things out?"

Inside, Jayde was crying. *No. I want to stay here. Please don't let me go.* But outwardly, she nodded. "Yes. They won't mind. Oh, and thank you for having your own pilot fly me to Kentucky. Wow. I've never flown on a private plane before."

He shrugged. "It's the least I can do."

She tried to smile, but it wouldn't hold on her face. "And thank you for this job. It really was the best one I've ever had. Except for that of being a self-employed artist, I mean."

He chuckled. "You're welcome. And congratulations, again, on your success."

Jayde swallowed, fighting tears. He really was going to let her leave. "Oh, yeah. I also wanted to thank you for setting up that wonderful art show for me. That went over great. I was really surprised."

"You were? I wasn't. I never doubted you for a minute. But all I did was make a phone call. Dirk did everything else. You ought to thank him."

"I did. He's been very kind. In fact, he gave me his card so I can call him when I get settled. In the meantime, he's calling other galleries and telling them about me. He says I can pretty much own the modern art world after yesterday's showing. It was his gallery's best ever."

"That's great. I couldn't be happier for you, Jayde. So, you're a wealthy woman now. How does that feel?"

"Well, I wouldn't say I was wealthy, exactly. But I can make my own way now."

"That's important to you, I know."

That's when she knew—he was giving her what she'd said she wanted...her freedom to be herself. He did love her. He did. Maybe if she talked long enough he'd cave or she would find the right words. "Yes, it is. I can spend most of my time painting now. Mr. Halliburton is even calling agents for me. And I'm grateful for that, too. So...everything should be okay."

"Good. That's all I ever wanted, Jayde...for you to be happy. Are you?"

She was certain her heart was in her eyes and denying everything she'd said before. "Yes?"

"That sounded more like a question."

She blinked. "Oh. No. It's not. I mean, yes."

"All right. Good. Well. If leaving makes you happy..." He paused, watching her. Jayde felt as if her very breath hung on his next words. He was going to ask her to stay, she just knew it. "Then, let's get to it. I'll get Lyle and—what's wrong?"

"Nothing." Stung, Jayde began gathering up her bags. Anger began to replace heartache. "I'll meet you at the front door."

"No. We can say goodbye right here. I won't be going with you to the airport."

She stopped and stared at him. "You won't?"

"No. I don't see much need. Do you?"

Anger fled. She wanted to die. "No. I suppose not."

He took a deep breath and crossed his arms. "That's what I thought. And I've got so much work to do here. I've really been putting it off for the past week. In fact, after you leave, I've got to pack, myself—"

"Where are you going?"

"Paris. You ever been to Paris, Jayde?"

"France? No. I've been to Paris, Texas, though. It's nice."

"I bet it is. But I meant France. You'd love it. It's a really artsy place."

"I've heard. Maybe I'll go there one day."

"You really ought to."

"I will."

"Good. Are you sure you're okay, Jayde? You look...I don't know...sad. Or upset."

"I'm fine."

"Okay. Good. Well, this is it then." He came over to her and gave her a quick hug, then said, "I appreciate your working for me, Jayde. You did a great job. I'm glad you had a chance while you were here to make a success of yourself. I know how much that means to you—more than anything else in your life."

She panicked. "No! Not more than anything else—"

But he was gone. It was over. He hadn't even helped her with her bags. Jayde stood there, staring at the empty doorway and tears pricked her eyes. She couldn't seem to make herself leave. She frowned. Was that the point—she couldn't leave because she was supposed to stay and fight for this love she felt? After all, Brad was just giving her a dose of her own medicine. He was allowing her to see how it would feel to live without love, to have nothing to fight for.

Just then, she heard Lyle's voice. He was speaking abnormally loudly. "Uh-oh, boss, sorry. There's something wrong with the limo. It won't start."

Jayde caught her breath. Excitement beat in her heart. Fate had stepped in. She couldn't leave if the car wouldn't start—

"Take the Jaguar, then," Brad answered, dashing Jayde's hope.

"What?" Lyle said, sounding confused. "But I thought—"

"Take the Jaguar."

She didn't hear anything for a moment…then, "Uh-oh, boss, we can't leave the house. The doors are all locked. That darned JOCK."

Again Jayde grinned, biting at her bottom lip. JOCK didn't want her to leave, either.

"Open the doors, JOCK."

"But, Mr. Hale," JOCK's electronic voice sounded. "I was under the impression that we—"

"No. Open the doors. Now."

"As you wish, sir."

Jayde exhaled, her hopes again dashed. Just then, Lyle filled the doorway. He looked as sad as she felt. "You ready, Jayde?"

She nodded. "Yes. If you'll just help me with my bags."

"Sure." He came over and grabbed them, then

turned to her. "Hey, listen. I thought this would end differently."

She shrugged. With Lyle, whom she thought of as her friend, there was no sense pretending otherwise. "Me, too. But I suppose it's just not in the cards."

His lips pressed together, Lyle moved aside, indicating she should precede him. "There was really nothing wrong with the limo. We'll take it to the airport."

Jayde frowned in confusion, then she understood. "Oh. A delaying tactic. I see. Thanks."

"You're welcome."

He sounded mad. Jayde turned to look at him. "Are you all right, Lyle?"

"I'm fine. But I know someone who isn't."

Jayde didn't say anything, but she felt certain he meant Brad. On her way out the front door, Jayde paused and turned...Brad wasn't there. Holding back her tears, she said, "See you, JOCK."

"See you, Mrs. Hale—I mean, Ms. Greene. You're the nicest human I know."

She chuckled, to keep from crying. "Thanks, JOCK. You're the nicest artificial intelligence I know."

With that, Jayde left. Seated in the back seat of the limo, she turned and looked out the car's back window. She couldn't be sure, but she thought she saw Brad standing in the house's front window. She waved, but she knew, with the car's tinted windows, that he couldn't see her. She kept looking over her shoulder, hoping Brad would stop them...until they turned the corner and she could no longer see the house.

SEATED IN the music room, listening to the Three Tenors, Brad was ready for Lyle when he got back from the airport.

The front door slammed. "He's in the multimedia room," JOCK said.

In only seconds—no doubt, Lyle had taken the stairs two at a time—the chauffeur was standing in front of Brad.

"What the hell's going on, boss? I thought we had a plan. I thought—"

"We did."

"Well, you sure as hell didn't stick to it. She's gone."

Smiling, happy, Brad stood up. "She is? Are you sure?"

"Well, I put her on the plane myself and closed the door. And Joe was taxiing down the runway, the last I saw them."

"Good." Brad stretched his muscles, noted Lyle's accusing stare. "What?"

Lyle suddenly sat down heavily, his head in his hands. "Man, I don't get any of this." He looked up. "I thought you love her."

"I do."

"Well, she loves you, too."

"I know."

"She didn't want to leave."

"I know that, too. But she wouldn't say it, would she?"

"I guess not. I wasn't actually listening…"

"Well, if you had been, you'd have heard her pride get in the way, just like mine was doing yesterday."

"So, you love her but let her go because she's got pride?"

"You could look at it that way."

"That doesn't seem right, boss. What about our plan to say the cars wouldn't work and having JOCK lock up the house?"

Brad chuckled. "That was your plan. It was a good one as far as it went. But I guess I wasn't willing to place so much on chance—the chance that she'd do exactly what she did. Stick to her story and leave."

Lyle was now absolutely beside himself. "But she did leave. And you let her."

"By all appearances, yes."

Lyle stood still…and really stared at Brad. "What are you saying?"

"I'm saying I know she loves me and that she didn't want to leave. I'm saying she didn't have the guts to fight for that love. She was painted in one corner. And I was painted in another. Just like in business. And like you said yesterday, I'm a risk taker."

Lyle threw his hands up. "I don't get it. You lost. It was that stupid idea of mine. I feel terrible."

Brad chuckled again. "Hold on, Lyle. No, I didn't lose. Because just like in business—and this is the secret behind my success, Lyle—I put it all on the line, but I also hedged my bet." He couldn't help it, he laughed happily.

"You've lost your mind, boss. What are you talking about?"

Brad signaled for Lyle to follow him. "Come on. I'm all packed."

Lyle walked alongside him. "Where we going?"

"*We're* not going anywhere. I'm going to Paris. I need you to drive me to the airport. And then I'd like you to stay here and be my house sitter for a while. And have Marta and Tony stay here with you, if you can get her to agree. You need some time together, you and your wife and son.''

Lyle stopped. A look of incredulity captured his broad face. ''You mean that, boss? She isn't really my wife anymore.''

''Well, maybe she will be, again, if you and I stay home a little more. Like you said, we're getting too damn old to be chasing around the world.''

''This is great. But what about you, boss? You're alone.''

Brad shook his head. ''No, I'm not. I'm going to Paris.''

''Wait. You can't go to Paris this evening—unless you're going commercial.''

''I'm not going commercial.''

''But Joe's flying Jayde back to Kentucky. I put her on the plane myself.''

Brad leaned back against the wall, smiling. ''Yes, you did.''

''Then I don't get it. You're going to Paris and Jayde's going to Kentuck—'' Lyle's expression went blank.

Brad grinned. ''Yes? Jayde's going where?''

''Jayde's going to Paris with you, is she?''

Brad pushed away from the wall and gave Lyle a high five. ''You got it, my man.'' He headed for his bedroom. ''Come on. Help me with my bags. Joe's stalling her until I get there.''

Lyle followed along behind his boss. ''She's going to kill you.''

Brad shrugged. ''Maybe. But would you like to bet on it?''

''Hell, no,'' Lyle said.

But JOCK got in the last word. Over the intercom, he played an instrumental version of "April in Paris."

No one seemed to mind that it was still only January. They were all in love. And it felt like April.

Epilogue

BY THE TIME Jayde and Brad arrived back in Florida from Paris—France—it was really April and they were more in love than ever. They were also married—really! Jayde's happy realization of her pregnancy had necessitated that informal ceremony in mid-February. The marriage rites had taken place in a small but picturesque chapel in the South of France, with only two strangers as their witnesses. Even now the memory of it made her smile. And hopefully, the baby would be a little early, so as not to generate a bunch of questions from her mother.

Jayde couldn't believe what her life had become in the past few months—all because she'd accepted her dream job. And she finally had a *real* wedding to celebrate. They were repeating their vows so her family would finally see her married. It didn't matter that they thought she'd married Brad in Las Vegas, not in Paris. So with her mother's excited and fluttery help, she donned a white wedding gown.

"Hold still, baby. There must be a million of these here tiny pearl buttons. Can you suck in some, Jayde? I believe you're already putting on some baby weight. You still taking those French vitamins?"

Her mother was leery of foreign things. "The vitamins aren't French, Mama. The doctor was. She said they're the same ones I'd get here, and that's what my doctor here said, too. So, yes, I'm taking them.''

"Well," Maxine Greene muttered, yanking Jayde around as she fought the buttons, "who knows? That baby might come out speaking some crazy foreign tongue. You know, this baby is the greatest present you and Brad could give us, honey. We didn't need a big new house back in Kentucky like the one you two bought us.''

"It was our pleasure, Mom. I'm just glad Daddy likes the new car, too. You can sure use a minivan, what with all the kids.''

"That reminds me. There. I'm done. Now I'm going to go check on your father and the boys. They'll make the cutest ushers. Then I still have to tackle your sisters' hair, if you want presentable bridesmaids, that is.'' She stalked toward the door. "No one in this family can do a single thing without me.''

Jayde knew the truth of that. *Let's see,* she pondered as she gathered up the yards of satin material of her beautiful gown and walked carefully over to the open French doors onto the balcony in their bedroom, *how did all this happen?*

Once outside, she gripped the balcony railing and stared out at the blue water. A string quartet was setting up and the caterer was arranging the white-clothed tables below. Flowers and satin streamers were everywhere. This wedding was for the sake of family and friends. And this time Jayde could actually wear a wedding gown. Better still, they *both* had wedding rings.

And this is the third wedding, right? She was losing count. The first one was in Las Vegas—the one her parents thought was the real one—which made this third one seem like only the second one and a recommitment ceremony. The second one, in France, was actually the first one, the one no one else knew about, but the one she and Brad would always celebrate privately. And now the third one was being shared with Lyle and Marta…who believed this to be Brad and Jayde's first wedding.

Jayde chuckled. *Dear God. Let's hope our guests don't start talking.*

Lyle had been in touch over the course of their European stay and had broken the good news to them about him and Marta in early March. When Brad had suggested a double wedding in April, Jayde had agreed. So, here they were.

Obviously, getting remarried every few months was going to be a family tradition with them. So, with that settled, the plans were begun and everyone who needed to be there had been flown in, including Jayde's entire family, Aunt Wanda and her bloat medicine, and believe it or not, Lucinda Kingston of Your Dream Job Employment Agency. Lucinda had even been asked to be Jayde's maid of honor. Brad had called her from Paris to thank her for sending him Jayde and she had broken down and apologized for her behavior. Now they were all friends. In fact, Lucinda had flown in early to make all the arrangements for today, and she'd done such a good job, that Jayde was thinking of asking her to be her personal secretary. Now, wouldn't that just be her dream job? Jayde meant that sincerely, too.

''Ah, 'tis Juliet my eyes behold upon yon balcony!''

Jayde blinked and looked down on her, well, husband-father of her baby-groom-boss—he never had

terminated her employment, after all. Her heart filled
with love. "I don't think those are the bard's exact
words, my love."

"Good." He put his hands to his waist. "Then I'm
not guilty of any copyright violations, am I?" He
looked her over. "You look very beautiful in that
gown."

Jayde wadded up a handful of the expensive and
luscious material. "What? This old thing?" Then she
quirked a grin, a secret smile only he would understand. "It's not good luck to see your bride before
the ceremony, you know."

He winked at her. "Which ceremony would that
be?"

Jayde put a finger to her lips. "Shh! Someone
might hear you."

"Someone like me, for instance?" This was JOCK.

"Ahh, JOCK, my man," Brad called out cheerily.
"You all ready to be best man for me and Lyle?"

"Yes," JOCK sighed. "Would you believe some
obnoxious child actually taped a black satin bow tie
to my control panel. I imagine I look quite spiffy.
And I've corraled another child to be the ring bearer
for me."

Jayde chuckled. "Now, JOCK, don't tell me you
don't like children."

"Oh, no," JOCK fussed. "I love children. What
choice do I have? Sadly, I've been reprogrammed to
do so."

"I see," Jayde said, winking down at her husband-
programmer. "Just like you were reprogrammed to
like me?"

Brad frowned up at her. "What are you talking
about?"

"Oh, don't play coy with me, Bradford Hale. JOCK told me how you reset him to like me."

Brad shook his head. "I did no such thing."

Jayde believed him. "You didn't? Then how—?"

Brad threw back his head and laughed. "I'll be damned. JOCK fell in love with you, too, Jayde. All on his own."

"I did no such thing," JOCK huffed. "I'm not capable of such piddling human emotions. Besides, I'm much too smart. For example, even now I'm only on the speakers here by you both. So what I'm going to say next will only be heard by you two." He then made a sound, remarkably like a throat being cleared. "My congratulations to you both. I'm honored to be your best man, although the choice was obvious. And finally...Mr. Hale, what are you doing outside and down there? Get up there on the balcony and kiss your bride-to-be...for the third time."

Modern Romance™
...seduction and
passion guaranteed

Tender Romance™
...love affairs that
last a lifetime

Sensual Romance™
...sassy, sexy and
seductive

Blaze™
...sultry days and
steamy nights

Medical Romance™
...medical drama on
the pulse

Historical Romance™
...rich, vivid and
passionate

27 new titles every month.

*With all kinds of Romance for
every kind of mood...*

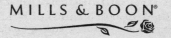

MILLS & BOON®

MILLS & BOON®

Modern Romance™

PREGNANCY OF CONVENIENCE by Sandra Field

A riveting read! When wealthy Cal Freeman invited Joanna on holiday, she knew he wanted a passionate affair. It was the perfect opportunity to secretly conceive her much wanted baby... But could she go through with her outrageous plan?

THE CONSTANTIN MARRIAGE by Lindsay Armstrong

Will they submit to their mutual desire?
Alex Constantin had agreed to a marriage of convenience with Tatiana Beaufort – but she surprised him on their wedding night by asking for a year's grace before making it a *real* marriage. Now, a year later, her enigmatic husband suggests they become lovers at last...

THE SECRETARY'S SEDUCTION by Jane Porter

From sensible secretary...to sexy siren!
Handsome business tycoon Morgan Grady proposes to the one woman he knows he can trust – his secretary Winnie Graham. But alone on his exotic private island, Morgan discovers that Winnie's composed exterior hides a storm of passion...

BLIND-DATE BRIDE by Myrna Mackenzie

Three proposals in two weeks?
When Lilah Austin turns to billionaire Tyler Westlake for refuge from the men sent by her matchmaking brothers, chivalry soon has him pretending that she's the love of his life. But faking it feels so real... How can Tyler convince Lilah that he's not merely *posing* as the perfect lover?

On sale 6th September 2002

*Available at most branches of WH Smith,
Tesco, Martins, Borders, Eason, Sainsbury's
and most good paperback bookshops.*

0802/01b

FREE!

2 Books
and a surprise gift!

We would like to take this opportunity to thank you for reading this Mills & Boon® book by offering you the chance to take TWO more specially selected titles from the Modern Romance™ series absolutely FREE! We're also making this offer to introduce you to the benefits of the Reader Service™—

- ★ FREE home delivery
- ★ FREE gifts and competitions
- ★ FREE monthly Newsletter
- ★ Books available before they're in the shops
- ★ Exclusive Reader Service discount

Accepting these FREE books and gift places you under no obligation to buy; you may cancel at any time, even after receiving your free shipment. Simply complete your details below and return the entire page to the address below. *You don't even need a stamp!*

YES! Please send me 2 free Modern Romance books and a surprise gift. I understand that unless you hear from me, I will receive 4 superb new titles every month for just £2.55 each, postage and packing free. I am under no obligation to purchase any books and may cancel my subscription at any time. The free books and gift will be mine to keep in any case.

P2ZEB

Ms/Mrs/Miss/Mr ....Initials..
BLOCK CAPITALS PLEASE

Surname...

Address...

....

....Postcode ....

Send this whole page to:
UK: The Reader Service, FREEPOST CN81, Croydon, CR9 3WZ
EIRE: The Reader Service, PO Box 4546, Kilcock, County Kildare (stamp required)